PRAISE

MW01135278

"The romance is well written different aspects of Amish and spite being part of a series, this book stands alone and is the type I like to curl up in front of the fire with on a cold winters day."

—Orchid, book reviewer for Long and Short Reviews
AMISH BABY SNATCHED, Book 1 in The Bishop's Daughters

"AMISH BABY SNATCHED is another captivating and heartfelt story by Diane Craver in her new series, The Bishop's Daughters. Diane has written this book with such depth that it is not your typical Amish inspirational book of romance and Amish life.

—Marilyn Ridgway, book reviewer, 5 stars

"This award recognizes outstanding writing styles in all book types and genres. Your book has received this award because I feel it is above and beyond a 5 Cup Rating."

—Matilda, for Coffee Time Romance & More
A JOYFUL BREAK, Book 1 in Dreams of Plain Daughters Series

"JUDITH'S PLACE provides readers with an inside look at the Amish community that is more in depth than other Amish books that I've read . . . It wasn't a sappy story, the tension and anxiety was real. A delightful book that I didn't want to put down. I loved the story and the depth of the characters."

—Robin Roberts, book reviewer for Once Upon A Romance
Book 2 in Dreams of Plain Daughters Series

"This was another enjoyable story in the Dreams of Plain Daughters Series. I loved the complexity Ms. Craver wove with these characters and her storyline."

—Diana Coyle, book reviewer for Night Owl Romance Reviews
Top Pick, 5 stars on FLEETING HOPE, Book 3

"Violet and Luke were extremely likeable characters and I felt the highs and lows they both were experiencing along the way while courting each other. . . I always enjoyed Ms. Craver's Amish stories because they each contained characters that were fully believable and you can't help but become invested with each storyline . . . I feel this is a wonderful series to enjoy in its entirely. I highly recommend this author and this series!"

—Diana Coyle, book reviewer for NOR Reviews
Top Pick, 5 stars on A DECISION OF FAITH, Book 4

"This book was realistic and emotional. All the characters played dynamic parts in the story. I recommend this book to everyone. I certainly enjoyed reading this author."

—Brenda Talley, book reviewer for The Romance Studio
5 stars, MARRYING MALLORY

"The author addressed some very tough issues in this book, including the loss of a child, eating disorders and post-abortion syndrome. Diane Craver discusses these topics with detailed professionalism. In a beautiful and sensitive way, she crafts advice, help and caring for the wounded souls. A job well done!"

—Shauna, book reviewer for The Long and Short Reviews
5 stars, WHEN LOVE HAPPENS AGAIN

"Ms. Craver's NEVER THE SAME is a heartfelt story about two families whose lives will intertwine for the rest of time. I loved the realistic characters and I constantly felt as if I were right in the room with them watching everything as it evolved. It was wonderful to read a story about something that could actually take place; a tale that, with its believability, could draw me in so deeply. This book is for my keeper shelf. Thank you, Diane Craver."

—Shayla, book reviewer for Romance Junkies
4.5 Blue Ribbon for NEVER THE SAME

"I really enjoyed this book. Diane Craver's casual and engaging style brought the characters to life. She did a wonderful job of capturing the beautiful, and sometimes touchy, relationship between sisters. The romance was heartfelt, and I was especially happy in the end when Whitney chose the guy I hoped she would."

—Shawna Williams, Inspirational Writer
5 stars, WHITNEY IN CHARGE

". . . it's not the classic chick-lit book. It has more depth than that... I believe there are a lot of different types of secrets in A Fiery Secret. Some are evil, some are wrong and some are through choice. It is a sweet, modern romance where the normal everyday complications of life meet a mystery head on. But above all, this book has a nice feel good ending that makes you smile."

—Janet Davies, book reviewer for Once Upon A Romance
4 stars, A FIERY SECRET

"Although this story takes place in the 1950s, I think it has a timeless feel to it and a message that lasts a lifetime. I have not decided if this is a good thing or a bad thing... it is so well written and the descriptions so authentic. This is truly an inspiring story for readers, young and old alike.

—Venus, book reviewer for Coffee Time Romance
4 stars, A GIFT FOREVER

A Plain Widow

ALSO BY DIANE CRAVER

Amish Fiction
The Bishop's Daughters Series
Amish Baby Snatched

Dreams of Plain Daughters Series
A Joyful Break
Judith's Place
Fleeting Hope
A Decision of Faith

An Amish Starry Christmas Night
An Amish Starry Summer Night

Christian Romance
Marrying Mallory
When Love Happens Again

Chick-Lit Mystery
A Fiery Secret

Contemporary Romance
Whitney in Charge
Never the Same
The Proposal
Yours or Mine

Historical and Christian Fiction
A Gift Forever

Visit Diane Online!
http://www.dianecraver.com

A Plain Widow

The Bishop's Daughters
Book Two

By

Diane Craver

DEDICATION

For my beloved sister,
Lois LaWarre
who has a generous heart and a fun spirit

But those who hope in the Lord
will renew their strength.
They will soar on wings like eagles;
they will run and not grow weary,
they will walk and not be faint.

Isaiah 40:31 (NIV)

NOTE TO THE READER

The Amish community I've created is fictional, but exists close to Wheat Ridge, which is an actual Amish community in the southern part of Ohio. Before I started writing my Amish series, I did extensive research to portray this wonderful faith as accurately as possible. I've used many rules and traditions common to the Amish way of life. However, there are differences between the various groups and subgroups of Amish communities. This is because the Amish have no central church government; each has its own governing authority. Every local church maintains an individual set of rules, adhering to its own *Ordnung*.

If you live near an Amish community, actions and dialogue in my book may differ from the Amish culture you know. The Amish speak Pennsylvania Dutch with variations in spelling among the many different Amish and Mennonite communities throughout the United States. I have included a glossary for the Pennsylvania Dutch words used in this book.

Many Amish mothers use disposable diapers. However, if you live near the Swartzentruber Amish, you will see cloth diapers flapping on their clotheslines. They also do not have indoor plumbing and do not use gas powered appliances. The very conservative Swartzentruber Amish emphasize tradition and resist change more than the majority of Amish groups. They differ from the Old Order Amish I write about in my books.

In spite of the differences among the various Amish communities, none have electricity in their homes, and they don't drive vehicles.

Pennsylvania Dutch Glossary

ach: oh

aenti: aunt

appeditlich: delicious

boppli: baby

bruder: brother

daadi: grandpa

daed: dad

danki: thank you

dat: father

dochder: daughter

ehemann: husband

Englisher: a non-Amish person

fraa: wife

froh: happy

frolic: a time for adult sisters or friends to get together to visit with each other while doing chores such as canning food, cleaning house and more.

Grossdaadi Haus: a smaller house that is connected to or nearby the main house, much like an "in-law suite."

gut: good

Gut nacht: good night

lieb: love

kaffi: coffee

kapp: prayer covering

kinner: children

mamm: mom

mammi: grandma

nee: no

onkel: uncle

Ordnung: Set of rules for Amish and Old Order
Mennonite living.

rumspringa or rumschpringe: running around; time before an
Amish young person officially joined the church, provides a
bridge between childhood and adulthood.

schee: pretty

schweschder: sister

wunderbaar: wonderful

ya: yes

CHAPTER ONE

As Molly Ebersol held her small son, Isaac, she stared at the hundreds of Amish and English men building a new barn. Sadness filled her soul that Caleb wasn't present to be part of it. In the past, he had helped build barns for others in their communities. If only Caleb had listened to her when she'd told him not to go in their burning barn, he would be alive now. Instead, Caleb died a month ago while trying to save their newly purchased horses. The love of her life was gone, which was terrible enough, but now her son and unborn baby would be fatherless.

Her white-haired grandmother reached for Isaac. "Let me take the boy."

A couple of weeks ago, Grandma Mary Sue and Grandpa Ray Bontrager had moved in with her. No one wanted her to live alone with nineteen-month-old Isaac, especially in her condition. She appreciated them leaving Florida early to stay with her. For the first time, her grandparents had rented a small house in Pinecraft for three months because both wanted to go where it was warmer in the winter. Pinecraft was a small neighborhood community of Amish and Mennonites outside Sarasota. It was a popular spot for the Amish farmers to visit during the winter when they didn't have as much outside work to do. Her grandfather said leaving the cold weather had helped to lessen his arthritic pain.

She kissed Isaac's forehead before handing the toddler to the older woman. "*Danki, Mammi*. He was getting heavy."

"I'll put him down for his afternoon nap." *Mammi* glanced down at the tired toddler. "Would you like me to read you a book?"

Isaac smiled, showing his dimples.

"I take that for a yes." Molly touched the older woman's shoulder. "I don't know what I would do without you. You're such a blessing to me."

Her grandmother laughed. "I had to come here when you wrote me how several families wanted you to live with them."

"I really didn't want to live with any of them, but I couldn't hurt anyone's feelings either by choosing one." Molly shrugged. "Besides, I want to always stay in the home I shared with Caleb."

After her grandmother and Isaac quietly left the kitchen, Molly thought how there might be a time when she could no longer afford to stay in her home. She overheard Deacon Levi Lantz tell another man how replacing the burnt barn would help her sell the property. It made her angry to hear the comment. Levi's wife had died five months ago, and he remained in their house with his four children. No one expected him to move but, of course, he was able to farm his property. She could rent out the acres to a farmer and share the crop profits, but there was a worry it could be another poor income year. The crops hadn't done well last harvest because of too little rain. She hoped and prayed this wouldn't happen again this year. How could she ever move from the place where she'd been happy and so in love? It had been her home with Caleb and Isaac.

When she heard the door open, Molly turned her head and saw her *mamm* entering the kitchen.

After removing her black bonnet, Lillian King's white *kapp* was lopsided on her head, and strands of auburn hair rested against her cheeks. As she put her bonnet and jacket on pegs, she said, "It surely is a blessing that someone donated the food for the workers. I wonder who could have been so generous."

Molly frowned. "I wish we knew so I could thank them. Martha Weaver said there was a note with the money but no name. Also the note left at the lumberyard wasn't signed either. I still can't believe how they left enough money for the lumber needed for the barn and even covered money for the cement expense."

"If it would have just been the food donation, I'd have suspected Martha and Robert covering the expense. Jacob said he saw the two notes, and it was the same handwriting on both. And, of course, it's not from our community. Your *daed* was going to give money from our church fund, but suddenly money appeared from an anonymous person." Her *mamm* tucked her loose hair back under her kapp before straightening the covering.

"I wish the person had just given it directly to *Daed* for our community fund. Then we would know who it was."

Mamm pulled a chair away from the table. "You need to sit. You have to be tired with that growing baby inside you and taking care of Isaac."

Molly thought, *Mamm and I both know the main reason I am exhausted all the time. Losing Caleb has completely drained my spirit.* Walking away from the window, Molly took her mother's suggestion and sat on the chair. Touching her expanding stomach, she said, "Violet wants me to go to the office sometime for an ultrasound. Personally, I think it's a little early for that. I'm only four months pregnant." Molly didn't add that it would be another medical expense. None of the Amish had medical insurance and took care of their own when necessary.

"After delivering Isaac in a car on the side of the road, I think that might be a good idea." *Mamm* grinned. "Who would have thought your baby would be the first one Violet would deliver? She did a great job and she wasn't even a midwife yet."

Molly nodded. "I know and I wasn't nice to her before that. I'm ashamed that I asked Caleb to go to the buggy shop to talk to Luke about breaking up with Violet." She remembered how Caleb hadn't wanted to go talk to Luke, but she had insisted. Luke and she had always been close with being the two oldest in their family. When he started dating Senator Robinson's daughter, Violet, Molly became afraid that her brother would leave their faith to become English.

"Your father and I didn't want Luke dating an Englisher either, especially a famous senator's daughter. Remember how I tried to fix Luke up with Katie Weaver. Your dad stewed about his relationship with Violet until she took the bullet meant for Luke."

"I should've saved Caleb's life. I wanted to go after him, but was stopped by a firefighter."

"It's good you were stopped. You might have lost the baby or left Isaac an orphan. I'm thankful each day that you didn't die too." *Mamm* poured a cup of coffee. "Would you like some coffee? It's a lovely day outside for March but still chilly."

Looking closely at her mother, Molly said, "I already had a cup this morning. I don't want to overdo on the caffeine." Should she mention to her parent about what seemed to be happening in their family? Her mother always managed to make people feel better and was such a good listener. Right now, she needed to vent and hear her mother's down to earth advice. "*Mamm*, why do you think so many bad things are happening to us? My *ehemann* was killed in a fire caused by an arsonist. Beth's firstborn, Nora Marie, died in her womb. Then she and Henry were happy to adopt Chloe's baby girl, Emma, but look how that turned out."

Leaning against the counter, *Mamm* said gently, "I wish with my whole being that Caleb hadn't died."

"I miss him so much."

"I wish I could take your pain away but I can't." *Mamm* paused for a moment, appearing to be deep in thought. "I think in Beth's situation, things have turned out fine. It was heartbreaking for them to lose their first child. In spite of my sadness at Nora Marie's death, I felt a strong spirit in the hospital room and knew it was God's love reaching out to me. I'm glad we were able to see her after she was born. And sure Emma was kidnapped, and scared all of us . . . but she was quickly found. It seemed unfair that Chloe decided to take Emma back, but Beth and Henry are blessed with expecting twins."

Molly sighed. "It just seems like we never had any tragic things happen, but now we do. It's not fair I lost Caleb. And he didn't die from some terminal disease. He was healthy and too young to die. To think some cruel person started the fire seems unbelievable. Why did they decide to burn our barn? I hope they find him and he goes to jail for a long time."

Her mother walked to her and gave her shoulder a squeeze. "I don't know why this had to happen to you. We all loved Caleb. He was a *wunderbaar* husband, father, and son-in-law. We never know what is going to change in our lives. Poor Levi lost his wife and now has four children to raise."

It was sad their deacon lost his wife, but she didn't want to talk about Levi. "I'm surprised you took the day off from teaching." Her mother enjoyed teaching at their Amish school. After Ruth Yoder resigned to marry David Hershberger, her mother had taken the first four grades while Judith Hershberger taught fifth through eighth grade. Molly thought it was romantic how her bishop father missed his wife while she was at school. It was obvious to all their children how much he loved their mother. Sometimes he drove the buggy to school so he could have lunch with her.

Eyeing a plate of cookies, her mother returned to the counter and finally took a snickerdoodle. "I always seem to like something sweet with my coffee." Putting the cookie on a napkin, she walked to a chair by the table. "Judith offered to take my class. I'm going to miss her when she gets married."

"I'm surprised she and Jacob haven't tied the knot yet." Judith and Jacob had been dating for three years. "Is it because she loves teaching so much that she put off getting married?"

After sitting, *Mamm* sipped her coffee. "She hadn't wanted to get married the same year Ruth married her dad. And apparently Jacob wanted to pay back some of the loan his dad gave him for the Graber's farm before they got married. And Violet asked Judith to be an attendant, so she'd have one relative in her wedding. But the waiting will soon be over for them. They plan on getting married sometime this spring."

"Violet was such a beautiful bride. Getting married the end of October turned out to be the perfect time for them." Molly recalled how it had been a gorgeous fall day. Even though the number of guests were huge, the Robinsons had managed to keep the wedding date a secret from the news people. Her father had been relieved that the wedding hadn't been attended by any TV reporters. They'd already had enough excitement from the kidnapping of Emma earlier that month.

Mamm nodded. "As soon as they were both baptized last fall, Luke said they were not waiting any longer. Violet looked lovely in her purple wedding dress. It was nice they went to Gatlinburg for a short honeymoon. Your *daed* grumbled a little about them going on a honeymoon, but some couples do go on a trip after they help clean up after the wedding. Violet will be busy with delivering a lot of babies the next several months. She might not get to see her new husband very much. It's seems there are a lot of Amish women in the family way. I hope Ada can help with some of them. I'm afraid many will want Violet to be their midwife since then a doctor won't need to be present at the home birth. It's too bad Ada isn't a certified nurse-midwife."

"I want Violet to deliver my baby." Molly smoothed her apron over her black dress, remembering how Luke had invested in Caleb's horse farm. They never would've gotten it started without Luke's help, but now she wished he hadn't helped them. Caleb might still be alive if he hadn't worried about getting the horses out of the barn.

She should be happy for her brother that he and Violet were finally married. Yet, it was hard to be happy about anything . . . except for Isaac. He was such a wonderful child. Why couldn't Caleb have thought about his family before rushing into the barn to save the horses? He was thrilled about her pregnancy and their family should have come first to Caleb. He never should have broken out of her grasp.

Touching her stomach, Molly wanted to cry but had to be strong. "I guess I should go outside to thank the workers."

"After I finish my cookie and coffee, I'll go and bring you back something to eat. They still have a few hours left of daylight to work. The wood frame structure will be done today." *Mamm* sipped her coffee and took another bite of cookie. "I'll check the coffee carafes to see if any need to be refilled. I'm glad Sharon thought to loan us several insulated carafes."

"I should help."

"You can eat first. There isn't much to do except put more food on the tables when the men are ready to eat again. Martha and Katie did a great job getting the food ready. They brought enough coolers and baskets of food for the whole day."

"What about the rest of the week when they come to finish the barn?" Although there seemed to be a common belief among Englishers that they did the whole job of building a barn in a day, it was definitely not true. Unfortunately, she'd have people around for a week to finish the barn. She'd be relieved when the barn was finished.

"Sharon Maddox and Ruth have offered to furnish food for the other days."

"It's nice that many English men came today to help get the frame up." Molly had been surprised to see several vehicles pull into the driveway. She knew the majority of people in Fields Corner liked having their Amish businesses because it increased the number of tourists for the town. However, there were a few English individuals who complained about the horses leaving droppings on the streets. These same people also voiced at the town meetings how inconvenient it was to be behind a slow-moving buggy when driving on the highways.

"Sharon's husband put the word out for help." *Mamm* stood and walked to the counter.

"It's something how Sharon is now friends with Ruth. I remember how close Irene Hershberger was to Sharon." Before Irene died from a heart attack, she loved visiting with her English neighbor, Sharon. Irene's husband, David, remained a widower for two years before marrying teacher Ruth Yoder. Well, she would never remarry. Caleb had been the only boyfriend she had ever wanted and loved. She couldn't imagine any man taking his place in her heart.

After her mother left, carrying the coffeepot, Molly stood and went to the counter. She took a wet dishrag and wiped up a spot of coffee on the counter. She needed something to do, and working on finishing her present quilt would be productive. Selling her quilts was the only thing she could think of to make money. She needed to earn an income before she had money coming in from the crops. She hated to leave the kitchen, though, since her mother planned to bring her something to eat.

Glancing out the window, she watched the men and how organized everyone was in building the barn. It was a *gut* thing to see them constructing her a new barn, but thought again how unfair that Caleb wasn't present to help. Exhaling a deep breath, she thought, *our marriage only lasted three short years. I wish we could have had a lifetime together. Meeting him at a volleyball game had been wonderful because he asked me if he could take me home in his buggy. I was surprised but pleased.*

A young woman, wearing blue jeans and a light jacket, hopped out of a car. When she saw it was Nicole Spencer, her spirits lifted slightly. The reason for meeting Nicole was sad, but the two women had hit it off immediately. Nicole had started her career as a firefighter, but now was the arson investigator for the county.

Molly opened the door and said, "Hi, Nicole."

Nicole quickly came to the doorway. "I had to come see you and see the barn raising. I've never been to one. I actually stopped in the driveway and watched it for several minutes. It's amazing to see so many men working together."

"I'm glad you came. I've thought of calling you." Molly knew Nicole had been trained at a state academy in how to gather evidence, analyze data, and determine the cause of a fire. She wondered if she had some news about the arsonist.

After entering the kitchen, Nicole gave Molly a hug. "How are you?"

Molly shrugged. "I'm still having trouble sleeping. And when I do finally go to sleep, I have nightmares of the fire. I hear the crackling noise of the flames and the horses' awful screaming. I call out Caleb's name and then I'm crying as I try to get to the barn. Usually at that point, I wake up and remember Caleb is dead."

"I'm so sorry. I can't imagine going through what you have had to deal with." Nicole's eyes filled with concern.

"Would you like something to eat or drink?"

"Your mother is going to bring me a piece of pie and coffee when she brings you something to eat. Your mom is a sweetheart." Nicole glanced around the kitchen. "Where's your adorable little boy?"

"He's with my grandma. Don't worry. I know you didn't just come to see me." Molly smiled. "And Isaac loves seeing you." Nicole loved holding and playing with Isaac. Pointing to the table, Molly said, "Let's sit and talk."

Nicole sighed as she pulled a chair away from the table. "I'll never get to babysit for you while your grandparents are here. Maybe you can take them with you when you go for your prenatal checkups. I can rearrange my schedule around your appointments."

Molly laughed, thinking how glad she was Nicole was visiting her. In spite of the reason they had met, she enjoyed her recent conversations with Nicole. She'd even thought of asking her father if she could have permission to have a cell phone for emergencies. It might be nice to call Nicole when she needed a driver for her pregnancy appointments. Or what if something happened to Isaac, and she couldn't get to the phone fast enough? Her grandparents wouldn't be here forever, Molly realized.

She shared a landline phone with her Amish neighbors. With the phone shanty being between the two properties, it took several minutes to get to it. The night of the fire, she hadn't needed to make the call herself because a neighbor had gotten up late at night to take pain medicine. When he saw the fire from his kitchen window, he'd gone to the shanty to call.

"You can visit anytime and play with Isaac. I'm trying to finish a quilt so I can sell it soon."

"Your quilts are stunning. I've been thinking about a good way to sell them. I thought of creating a website for you. I'll post pictures of your quilts, and we'll sell them online. I can get a free website."

"*Danki.* That's generous of you. I'll think about it. I don't see why that would be a problem with our church rules. Weavers have a website for their bakery and furniture store." Molly twisted a prayer tie and asked, "Are you sure you have time to do this for me?"

Nicole laughed. "I have plenty of time. I don't have a boyfriend so it will take my mind off not having a husband and children yet."

She remembered Nicole had mentioned how she was going to be twenty-nine soon and still had no serious boyfriend. It was hard to believe because Nicole was a lovely woman with blonde hair and green eyes. Molly grinned. "I know a few single men but you'd have to become Amish."

"I'll keep that in mind."

Pressing her hands together on her lap, Molly knew it was time to talk about Nicole's investigation. "Have you any leads to who started the fire?"

"I wish I could tell you that we arrested the person committing this tragic fire, but unfortunately, we haven't. None of your neighbors saw anything the night of the fire. The neighbor who called never saw any vehicle leaving the scene. I wish we had witnesses to the fire. I hate my investigation hasn't found anything new to report to you. Justin is also frustrated we haven't learned anything new. We won't give up until we catch the arsonist."

Detective Justin Benning was from the Adam County offices. He'd been kind to her but she had felt a bit uncomfortable with some of his questioning. She got the impression he'd been surprised she knew little about Caleb's life before he'd moved to Fields Corner. "I know you're doing your best. I just don't understand why someone did this to us." Who hated them enough to start a fire in their barn?

"Justin and I are going to talk to Caleb's parents again." Nicole tilted her head, giving her a thoughtful look. "I know I asked you this before but if you should think of anything at all that Caleb might have mentioned about his life before he moved here, that might help us."

"He lived in a small community close to Bethel with his parents before they moved here. A great-uncle left them his farm here in our district but you know that. Do you think someone from his past could have torched the barn?"

Nicole shook her head. "Probably not but we have to keep searching for answers. I will find whoever decided to torch your barn. This is a small community and I'm hoping somehow there will be a lead soon."

"I'm glad you're the investigator for this crime."

"Have you thought of anyone who had a grudge against Caleb?"

"No." Molly exhaled a deep breath. "I don't understand why someone would want to commit arson. Especially to us."

"An arsonist does it because it is their way of asserting themselves in a powerful way. Their own lives are powerless. We have thought your barn fire might be a hate crime against the Amish, but fortunately, there haven't been any more fires happening in your community."

"And I hope there won't be." Molly paused for a moment. "We did have someone in a white car honk their horn at us a couple of months ago. I didn't think to mention it before because sometimes the English drivers get impatient when they are stuck behind us and will beep their horns when they start to drive past us. But this particular time, the driver also yelled swear words at us and said that we should stay off the roads with our horses and buggies. He continued and said that the Amish caused accidents. We were afraid he was going to run us off the road because he kept his car next to our buggy for a few minutes. Thank goodness, another car came from the other direction, because then he went ahead of us."

"Did you see the driver?"

"I just noticed he had dark hair and he drove a white car. I can't imagine him starting the fire just because our buggy slowed him up for a minute." Twisting her prayer tie around her finger, she asked, "But do you think this driver could be the one who killed Caleb?"

"It's possible. If you see this car and driver again, try to get his license plate number." Nicole's jaw clenched. "I want to get this person and if he's the arsonist, I'll make sure he goes to jail for the rest of his life."

Chapter Two

Jonathan Mast hesitated before knocking on the widow's door. He'd helped with the framing of the new barn, but now the structure part was finished. Although Jonathan planned to return sometime during the week to help finish the barn, it seemed a good time to tell Molly Ebersol that he would be happy to plant her crops. Since he recently had bought a small farm nearby, it would be doable. It had to be difficult for her with a small child to cope with a farm, and he'd learned just today that she was in the family way. It wouldn't be good for her to have extra stress and to worry about money.

Sadness filled him at the memory of her tortured face. He was the firefighter who had held her back from rushing into the burning barn. Once he convinced her that he'd find her husband, she finally had stood still. As soon as he left her side and entered the barn, he had located her husband. After he'd quickly dragged Caleb Ebersol from the barn, Molly had rushed to her dead husband.

It'd been such a tragic fire. Not only a death of an Amish man, but all the livestock had perished too. Briefly, he thought how the week before the fire, he'd talked to Caleb about buying a draft horse from him. When he moved to the area, Jonathan heard excellent things about the horse farm.

As he raised his hand to knock on the door, Molly opened it. "*Ach*, hi," he murmured.

Giving him a startled look, she gave him a little smile. "*Danki* for your work on my barn. I'm on my way to look at it now. Is there something you need?"

Noticing how beautiful Molly looked with her bright blue eyes and auburn hair, he was speechless for a moment. "I wanted to tell you that if you need anyone to plant your crops this spring, I'll be happy to."

Molly gave him a focused glance without answering him. *She must be trying to figure out who I am. I doubt she remembers me from the night of the fire*, he thought. "I'm Jonathan Mast. I live just a couple of miles from here. I recently moved here and bought a farm."

A pained expression crossed her face and she said, "You are the firefighter who stopped me from entering the barn."

"*Ya*, I am. I'm sorry about your husband."

"I still can't believe he's gone. If only he hadn't gone back to get the horses. *Danki* for going inside the barn to try and save him."

"I wish I could've saved him. It was awful what happened." He didn't want to say it was God's will, because he didn't feel that was the best thing to say. She probably had heard this a lot from everyone. He was close enough that he could breathe in the sweet scent of her hair. He moved away from the door, so she'd have room to step down to walk to the barn.

"I'm sure you're anxious to get home after a long day here. You can walk with me to your buggy while I go look at the barn."

"I'm not in a hurry to get home. I was just moving out of your way so you can take a closer look at what was done today."

After they stepped off the porch, he said, "I was here a week before the night of the fire. I came to look at your husband's horses. He had such fine horses for sale. I was planning on buying a Belgian draft horse from him."

She stopped walking and stared at him. Why did he mention the horses? She didn't need a reminder of how all the horses died in the fire.

"Did you already pay him for the horse? I'll give you your money back."

"I hadn't given him any money. We shook hands on our deal. I planned on returning with the money."

She paused for a moment. "That's right. Caleb mentioned someone was going to buy a horse from him. It must have been you."

"I'm sorry. I shouldn't have mentioned it."

She shook her head. "It's okay. Caleb loved horses and was just getting his horse farm off to a *gut* start. He looked forward to when Isaac would be big enough to go to the horse auctions with him. He hoped our son would want to be involved in the horse business too."

"I'm sorry someone started the fire. If there is anything at all I can do, please let me know."

As Molly resumed walking, she said, "*Danki*. I'll talk to my grandpa about you helping with the crops. I'm sure he'll appreciate the help. Won't you be busy, though, with your own farm?"

"I only have a small farm. I didn't want too many acres because I work for a construction company. I enjoy working for them and building homes from the ground up. It's a *gut* place to work because I'm not the only Amish man. Our employer even has a van to pick us up."

She frowned. "I hate for you to have to take time off your job to plant my crops."

"It'll be fine with my boss. We do have some days off, depending on the weather and other things that might delay a house getting started. The foundation might not get started when expected, things like that."

He could tell Molly was in the family way, but didn't feel like he should ask when the baby was due. It seemed unfair that she had a little son plus a baby on the way, and no husband in the picture. Although she had family close by, he didn't want Molly to feel like she had to sell the farm right away. He recalled how when his older sister, Clara, lost her husband, she hadn't wanted to move back home. Keeping the farm for the first two years was important to her as a widow and a mother to three *kinner*, and by the time, she met her second husband, it was time for her to move on.

Now that they were by the barn, he grinned. "Well, what do you think? Are you going to fire me and the other men?"

"*Nee*. It looks perfect. I won't need to fire you."

"That's a relief because I'd hate for my construction owner to hear I got fired. He might decide I'm not good enough for his company."

She gave him a little smile and he realized how when Molly smiled, she was even more beautiful.

* * *

While Molly changed her son's diaper, she thought about Jonathan Mast, and how comfortable she felt talking with him. Her mother was right that he had probably saved her life by stopping her from entering the barn. She wouldn't have had the proper fire equipment on, and it'd been better that Jonathan went into the blazing barn to get her husband.

Suddenly she wondered if he wanted to help with farming her land because of guilt. Did he feel immense guilt that he hadn't saved her husband? However, there wasn't anything he could've done. Caleb was dead when he had found him.

Jonathan was the first Amish firefighter she knew in their district. Or, she thought he must live in their Amish community, now that he bought a farm nearby. *Since he's the only firefighter in our area, how does he get to the fires*, she wondered. There must be an English firefighter available to pick him up in case of a fire. It'd take too long to hitch a horse to a buggy to go to Fields Corner and to the surrounding areas of their small town.

Now that she thought about it, why weren't there other Amish volunteer firefighters in their town? She remembered a campaign several months ago to get more volunteer firefighters. She didn't recall any Amish man requesting to join the fire department. It was hard to know if her bishop father would mind having anyone in their church district becoming firefighters, since it apparently had never been an issue. *Well, if Jonathan starts attending our church Sundays, I'm sure it will come up sometime,* she thought.

After she fastened the tabs of the disposable diaper, Molly lightly put her head on his tummy. She was rewarded with his giggle and a smile. He was a little ticklish there but not as much as his father. "Your *daed* was so ticklish all over. I used to love to tickle him."

"Dada," Isaac said.

"You had a fine dada, Isaac. He loved you a lot. I'm sure he's watching us from heaven." Her throat thickened. Would Caleb be disappointed in her for staying in their home? Maybe he'd rather she lived with his parents, Rose and Andy. It might be wrong of her not to sell the house, but as the widow, she had to make the hard decisions. If she lived with Caleb's parents, her mother might be hurt. Also her sisters, Priscilla and Sadie, would love to have her living with them again. It just didn't seem like something she could do, but she would continue to pray about everything. *Maybe moving back to my childhood home will be something God wants me to do,* she thought.

Although it seemed like she had lived the life she was supposed to and married a fine Christian man, God still took him. It was hard not to be bitter some days, but she needed God in her life even more now with soon having to raise two *kinner* on her own. Well, not completely on her own. She had *wunderbaar* support from her family, but it was not the same as having Caleb in her life.

She finished putting a sleeper on Isaac. Instead of putting Isaac immediately in his crib, she sat in the rocking chair in his bed-room. Although he was worn out and he probably would've gone to sleep quickly by himself, she felt like holding him. He was such a cuddly child, and Molly loved how he rested his head against her chest. She wanted to enjoy this quiet time with him after a full day with people coming and going to work on the barn. Soon enough, Isaac would have to share her time and lap with the new baby.

As she rocked Isaac and held him close, she remembered the last day with Caleb. Their last hours together had been during a cold winter day. When they woke up very early as they always did, Caleb had pulled her into his strong arms and kissed her. He'd smiled and asked, "How's my beautiful wife?"

"I'm enjoying being in your arms. It's my favorite place in the whole world."

"Right answer."

Then he'd given her another long kiss before placing his hand on her pregnant belly. "I can't wait until I can feel this little one kicking. Having a baby is such a miracle from God. We're so blessed. I love you, Molly."

"I love you too," she'd replied.

"How about we go to Fields Corner for the noon meal?"

"I don't think we should spend the money."

He gave her an amused look. "I know you're eating for two, but I think I can afford a nice dinner for us. Anyhow, I have some great news. Someone is going to buy one of my horses later this week."

They'd gone to Angela's Restaurant for supper instead of going earlier. It'd been incredible and they'd laughed a lot. It was like a date even though Isaac was with them.

A bittersweet feeling rushed through her . . . glad she had a pleasant memory of their last evening together, but so heartbroken that there couldn't be more happy times. No woman should lose her husband after only a brief marriage.

Why couldn't God have given them a warning that some evil person wanted to hurt them? If only the bedroom windows had been opened, they might have heard the horses' screams before it was too late. She hoped the arsonist was caught soon and thrown into jail. Sure, it was the Amish's way to forgive. But it wasn't possible for her to feel anything, but hatred for the person responsible for Caleb's death.

CHAPTER THREE

Dr. Perry Knupp turned his headlights off before he pulled into the driveway. He didn't want Molly Ebersol or her grandparents to see his car. It was important that he remained anonymous.

When he'd helped with the barn raising earlier in the day, Perry felt relief when no one suspected he'd been the one to give the money for the barn and food expenses. But really, why would the Amish community think he was the one to donate the money? They wouldn't know about his connection to Caleb Ebersol. He wasn't the veterinarian for anyone's livestock in Fields Corner or the surrounding area. For years, veterinarian, Dr. Haney, had taken care of the livestock for the Amish and non-Amish farmers. Even though giving money for the food and lumber might seem generous enough, Perry knew better. It wasn't enough at all. Not when he suspected his younger sister, Stacie, had caused the fire tragedy.

When their parents had both passed, he took custody of fifteen-year-old Stacie. Ever since his wife, Kathleen, had died five years ago, Stacie had taken care of many household duties plus did the monthly invoice billing for his business. It'd been a blessing to have Stacie help with his young daughter, Mia, whenever he had to spend more time traveling to see his patients at farms. While he loved being a large animal veterinarian, it wasn't like being in a clinic and seeing small animals.

After Kathleen's sudden death from a car accident, he'd been in shock and a big emotional mess. Stacie was his anchor and he owed her a lot for putting up with him when he wasn't able to be much of a father to Mia.

Now Stacie needed him. Caleb had broken his sister's tender heart when he stopped being her fiancé. He'd always wondered if Stacie hadn't miscarried, if things might have been different. Once she told Caleb about the pregnancy, he'd proposed marriage to her. Sometimes he blamed himself for hiring Caleb as an assistant. Remembering how he liked Caleb on the spot, he had only checked one of his references. Although he had never worked for a veterinary clinic before, Caleb seemed like the right fit for his practice. Caleb's love of animals, his pleasant demeanor, and his muscular build were all things necessary for him to have in an employee. When Caleb went with him to the farms, he had been helpful each time.

Of course, he hadn't been happy when Caleb and Stacie said they were expecting a baby. They were not married for one thing and another reason was their lack of money. He considered offering them his basement for their living quarters. Before having a chance to say anything, Stacie lost the baby.

Only a month after this happening, Caleb told them both together that he was returning to his faith and moving to Fields Corner. It'd been a huge shock because he'd never mentioned being raised Amish, and he even had a truck. Why would he or Stacie have suspected Caleb of being Amish? He carried a cell phone, drove a vehicle, and never dressed like a Plain person.

He'd asked Caleb, "How can you go back to your Amish faith when you've been living as a non-Amish man? I've heard that the Amish shun a person when he has done the things you have experienced."

"I haven't joined the church yet. I was in what we call *rumspringa*. It's a time when some parents might look the other way while the young people experience some English things before joining our church. Not all the youth do what I have done. Some might just go to a movie or a baseball game. I wanted to get my high school diploma and see what it was like to drive. If I had been baptized, then shunning would've happened. I'm planning on taking instructions soon so that I can be baptized in the Amish church."

"You went way too far with Stacie. It's wrong how you've treated her and got her pregnant. I wish I had never hired you. You basically lied to me and to Stacie. You should have been upfront with us in the beginning. It's hard for me to believe you were raised Amish. You've been dishonest and haven't respected Stacie."

"You're right. I should have told you about my Amish background, but I wanted to work for you. I wasn't sure you'd hire me if you knew I wanted to try a new way of living."

"That wouldn't have made a difference to me. Amish are known for their hard work, but keeping something like this secret was wrong. If Stacie knew you had been Amish, she'd might not have gotten involved with you in the first place."

At this point in the conversation, he remembered Stacie's offer to attend Caleb's church with him to see if she could become Amish. Although he'd been surprised to hear Stacie considering this simple way of life, he realized then how deep her feelings were.

Stacie had touched Caleb's arm. "We can work everything out so we can be together."

Caleb sadly shook his head. "It's hard for an English person to become Amish after being raised with electricity and other worldly things. Very few people from your world can live a Plain life."

A few months later, Stacie had sobbed when she learned Caleb planned to marry an Amish woman. Perry couldn't believe Caleb had fallen in love that quickly with another young woman. He wondered if Caleb had ever truly loved his sister.

He hated himself for thinking Stacie had started the fire that caused Caleb's death, but many things pointed to her as the arsonist. On the day of the fire, Stacie was extremely jittery while billing his customers. He'd never seen her acting as if she was high on something. He'd told her to relax and asked what was wrong with her.

"Nothing's wrong. Oh, by the way, I won't be home tonight. I'm going to a movie with Charlotte."

That night his sister hadn't gone out with Charlotte because Charlotte had called to see if Stacie felt better. His sister had called off the movie because of illness. When she arrived home at one o'clock in the morning, Stacie had black smudges on her face and she smelled like smoke.

He couldn't chance asking Stacie if she'd set the fire because it'd be better in the long run if he didn't know for sure. What if she had done it? Then if the police found out he was aware of her crime, he could be charged for not sharing information about her. This way he could say that he hadn't known his sister had been the arsonist. Or what if he asked Stacie and she was innocent? She would be hurt deeply that he had even suspected her.

As he walked toward the front of the house, Perry thought, *I wish now I had tried to leave it yesterday, but it seemed dangerous to leave it on the front porch in broad daylight. Someone might have seen me do it. Leaving it in the mailbox wasn't a good option either. The money might have been stolen if I'd put it in the box.*

Now that he was on the front porch, relief went through him that Molly Ebersol didn't have a dog to alert her of his appearance. Everything was quiet and dark. It was fortunate that there were no outside lights. If Molly should wake up and peek out of a window, it wouldn't be good for her to see him leaving her property. The full moon lent enough light for him not to stumble and to see clearly the spot by the door. Leaning closer to the welcome mat on the porch, he dropped the manila envelope of money.

He ran back to his silver Toyota car and once inside, he pulled off the gloves he wore. *I probably didn't have to worry about finger-prints on the envelope. I don't have a police record. My prints wouldn't have been found, but it just seemed like a safe thing to do.* As he backed out of the driveway, he exhaled a deep breath. Once on the road, he turned on his headlights. Then he wondered if the enclosed note with the money was a bad idea. Well, he wasn't going back now to retrieve the note. Besides, he'd left notes with the other money he'd donated.

* * *

On Saturday morning, Molly poured a cup of coffee for her *daed*. "*Danki* for coming to work on the barn again and organizing the work crews." Molly appreciated her father speaking to the men yesterday before they'd left for the day. He asked which ones could work again, so they would know how many to expect.

Amos smiled at her. "I'm glad to help. Besides, I like to delegate jobs. I learned from your mother when I saw how well she doled out instructions for our *kinner* while you were growing up. Your coffeecake smells *appeditlich*."

"I made two of them and two loaves of banana bread. What time did you tell the men to come?"

"I told them at nine or soon after. Most are coming after they get their morning chores finished." Amos glanced at the wall clock. "It won't be long now."

Molly opened a cabinet drawer and removed two pot holders. Opening the oven door, she peeked at her baked items. After she removed the pans of bread, she placed them on metal racks to cool for a few minutes. "The bread is done but the coffeecake needs to bake a little longer."

"Where's my grandson?"

"He's upstairs with *Mamm*. He already ate his breakfast and she took him to change his diaper."

During their conversation, Grandpa Bontrager had entered the room. Each morning he liked to go for a walk. She knew it gave him something to do and thought again, how sad it was that they lost all their livestock. Otherwise, he would have been busy milking cows. He also would have been helping Caleb take care of the horses. But some cruel person had stolen the life she used to know and love from her and Isaac. Now everything was sad and different.

Molly glanced at her grandfather and noticed he had an envelope in his hands. "What do you have there? It's too early for the mailman to come."

"It wasn't in the mailbox. I found it on the front porch. Your name is on it."

She walked to him and he handed her the envelope. After opening it, she removed a bundle of money. "My goodness. This is a lot of money. And there's a note with it." She read out loud, "I'm very sorry for your heartbreaking loss. I wish the fire had never happened." Looking up from the note, she said, "There isn't a name included. I wonder if it could be the same person who gave money for the lumber and the food for the barn raising."

Her *daed* stroked his gray beard and frowned. "It could be, but why is this person or persons being so generous? Is it because it's someone who knows we don't have property insurance?"

Molly shrugged. "I can't imagine who it could be. I better tell Nicole about it."

Grandpa Bontrager went to the stove and picked up the coffeepot. As he poured coffee into his mug, he said, "I'm wondering if the person responsible for the fire is feeling sorry for everything. Maybe he is giving the money because of his guilt."

The oven timer went off so Molly laid the money and envelope on the table before turning the timer off and checking on the coffeecake. Smells of cinnamon and brown sugar from the freshly baked cake filled the air as she removed each Bundt pan.

After placing them on the counter, she turned to stare at both men. In a bitter voice, Molly said, "I hope it isn't, because I don't want their money. If they are trying to lessen their guilt, money isn't going to do it. I hope they find the person who started the fire. I don't know how anyone could have done something this terrible to Caleb. I thought everyone loved him."

"I can't think of anyone either who would do something like this," *Daed* said. "I wonder if one of the men here yesterday could have put it on the porch."

"I went out the front door last night for Molly, to see if there were any phone messages for us. I'm sure the envelope wasn't there then."

Molly sat down and twisted a prayer tie around her finger. "I remember that. He or she must have left it later. Probably when we were in bed and asleep because none of us heard anything."

Daadi sipped his coffee. "Molly, you might as well count the money."

After she separated the money into two piles of twenty and ten dollar bills, Molly counted one thousand dollars. "I didn't see the handwriting on the other notes, but I'm guessing it's the same person who donated money for the barn expenses. If it's a kind-hearted person and they didn't start the fire, why are they giving me money?"

"Maybe he doesn't have a family and what happened touched this person's heart. There are good people in the world," *Daed* said. "Look at all the men and women who came yesterday to work.

There were many English among us. I hope the giver of the money will be richly rewarded for his generosity. And it says in the Bible that we're to look after widows and their fatherless *kinner*."

Although she realized her *daed* referred to the verses in the book of James, she hated being reminded of being a needy widow. Molly shrugged. "I guess I can use the money to buy a horse. I don't like to be dependent on others all the time when I need to go somewhere. I'll need a buggy, too, but will get a used one. I definitely can't afford a new buggy."

"I'll work something out with Luke," *Daed* said. "I'm sure he'll give us the family discount when we buy a buggy from him."

"In that case, it's nice Luke is in the buggy business, but I don't want him to lose money by helping me." Molly thought how her brother wasn't a single man but married now. She didn't want him to cut the buggy price too much for her sake.

"That's what family does." *Daadi* patted her shoulder. "I can help pay for the buggy."

"*Danki*." Rising, she said, "I'll put the glaze on the coffeecakes while they are warm, then I'll go call Nicole and tell her about this money."

She remembered how Nicole mentioned doing a website for her quilts. Although she'd like to ask about having a cell phone for emergencies and her future quilt business, she decided it could wait. She'd only focus on the website. It was better with her father to focus on one thing she wanted. Glancing at her father, she said, "Nicole said she can make a website for me so I can sell my quilts. She would be in charge of it and she can get a free website.

Weavers have an online site for their furniture and bakery businesses."

"*Ya*, that might be okay to have a website for your quilts." Her *daed* chuckled. "I can tell you for sure after I eat a piece of your coffeecake."

As she held the bowl of glaze, Molly grinned at her father. "I better get the glaze on it then."

Chapter Four

It was the first time she'd attended church since being a widow. Well, actually she'd only missed two services since they didn't have church each Sunday. Like most Amish districts, they had church every other Sunday at someone's house or barn. Growing up, she'd loved how their house had a removable wall, which separated the kitchen from the living room in their split style farmhouse. Whenever they hosted the Sunday church service and singing, the wall was removed so a long open space existed. The area seated over a hundred people. Today church was at Samuel and Rachel Weaver's house. When Samuel had built the house for his bride, he'd put the removable wall in.

When she and Caleb had their Sunday turns in the rotation, they had held the services in their barn because there wasn't enough room in their house for everyone in their district. Even though they got a good deal when they bought the foreclosed house, barn and acreage, she wasn't thrilled with buying the property. Because of the lower price, she never mentioned to Caleb how disappointed she was in the house. The previous owners had started several projects in the home but never finished them. Another thing they had to do was to remove the electricity, and it cost too much in her mind. Caleb's dream had been to have a horse farm, so she understood that had to be a priority. Making improvements on the house had to wait until they had money.

Molly glanced at Rachel and Samuel's sister, Katie, and thought how nice it was that both women were pregnant. They had been best friends for years. Their mothers, Irene Hershberger and Martha Weaver, had also been good friends. If Irene had lived, she would have been thrilled that Rachel had married Samuel. Rachel's baby was due in October. Katie and her husband, Timothy, were expecting their first baby in September. Their beginning had been rocky because when Katie had expected to marry Timothy, he'd decided to leave their community to marry an English woman. He had a daughter with his first wife, but when she died in a car accident, he'd returned to his Amish faith. Katie Weaver had been terribly hurt by Timothy's actions. When he realized he had made a mistake in leaving her and Fields Corner, it hadn't been easy for him to convince Katie that he loved her. However, he adored his little daughter, Allie, and was thankful his wonderful child came out of his first marriage.

It had been a rocky start, too, for Rachel Hershberger and Samuel Weaver when a sudden death turned their lives upside down. Molly remembered how Rachel's mother, Irene, had only been in her forties when she'd died unexpectedly from a heart attack. Rachel and Samuel were planning to marry, but as the oldest daughter, she took over taking care of her younger twin brothers, Noah and Matthew. Because their other sister, Judith, was a schoolteacher, the cooking and most of the cleaning fell on

Rachel's shoulders. After two years of taking care of her father and siblings, Rachel wasn't sure if she wanted to join their church. Her mother shouldn't have died so young, and Rachel surmised that maybe it was too hard to be an Amish married woman. She also blamed her father for them not having a phone shanty. Her mother might have survived if she had received medical care quickly instead of waiting so long for the ambulance to arrive.

Fortunately, when Rachel left Fields Corner to go to Cocoa Beach with her Aunt Carrie and cousin Violet, she had the time to reflect and to pray. While on the beach, Rachel realized she needed to forgive her father. She no longer feared joining the church and knew marrying Samuel was the right choice. A miscarriage early in their marriage had crushed both Rachel and Samuel.

I hope everything goes well with this new pregnancy, Molly thought. *But if it doesn't, at least Rachel has Samuel. I'll have to give birth without Caleb at my side. Why did he have to go back to the barn? I told him not to. He should still be alive. God took him too soon.* Glancing around the women's side, she noticed the only other widows were middle-aged or older. It must be extremely hard for them not to have their husbands, but at least they had them longer than she had her Caleb. Tears sprang to her eyes and her chest hurt. *I should've made up an excuse and stayed home.* Seeing the young couples only intensified her loneliness. Loss still hung so heavy in her mind. She wished she could let it go, but it was with her constantly.

Her *schweschder*, Priscilla, nudged her side and whispered, "Molly, are you okay?"

"I'm missing Caleb," she whispered back. "I wish I had stayed home."

Priscilla squeezed her hand. "I'm sorry. The sermon should be over soon."

Molly nodded. "I'm glad both our ministers are healthy again, so Levi isn't preaching." When Levi had preached, church service had been longer than the usual three hours. Molly didn't understand why Luke always found Levi's sermons inspiring. She certainly hadn't been impressed with his long sermons. Fortunately, as a deacon, Levi had other duties so he was seldom asked to preach. With him being a widower and having four *kinner*, it was good he wasn't a bishop or a minister.

She swiped at her tears with a shaky hand. *I need to stop thinking about what I lost and concentrate on what I have—my sweet Isaac.* She leaned her head far enough so she could see around several women sitting between her and Grandma Bontrager. She wanted to see if Isaac was behaving for her grandmother. She'd offered to take him during the service. Her son slept on her grandmother's lap, so she couldn't use him for an excuse to escape the rest of the service. Gazing another moment at her son, she noticed how his blond hair was getting too long. She should give Isaac a haircut sometime. Caleb had mentioned that his hair had been blond as a child, but later became light brown. Isaac's eyes even reminded her of Caleb because they were pale blue instead of the deeper blue of her eyes.

* * *

After the church service ended, the men went to convert the benches into tables. Jonathan felt relief that plenty of men were doing this job, because he wanted to catch up with Molly. He knew she would probably help serve the noon meal. He should tell her he'd talked to her grandfather before church, and tomorrow they planned to get the fields ready for planting. When he saw Molly with her little boy, Jonathan rushed to her side.

He noticed her frown when she saw him. Maybe this wasn't a good time to talk to her. As he hesitated, he noticed how beautiful she looked but saw sadness in her luminous eyes.

"I'm glad you came to our church service," Molly said.

"Me too. I enjoyed the sermons." He smelled a scent of vanilla and strawberry, and wondered if it was the shampoo Molly used. Realizing he shouldn't be thinking of Molly's beauty and especially her hair, he took a breath. "I talked to your grandfather. I'm going to help him tomorrow with the plowing."

"*Danki* for your help. I need to talk to you for a moment about something serious. It can wait until tomorrow, but I'd rather we talk now if that is okay with you." She gave him a questioning look.

"Now is fine. Are you feeling okay?" Jonathan asked. "You seem distraught."

"It's the first time I've attended church without Caleb. I miss him so much."

"I'm sorry the fire happened and you lost your husband."

"I'm glad I have Isaac, but it's hard to know that he and my new baby will grow up without their father."

"I can't imagine what you're going through. I'll keep you in my prayers."

"*Danki.*" Molly cleared her throat. "When I saw you after church, I realized that you might be able to answer a question for me. I just want to take Isaac to Priscilla while we talk." Molly pointed to a younger woman just a few feet away from them. She glanced down at her little boy and asked, "Would you like to see *Aenti* Priscilla for a moment? I'm sure she'll give you something yummy to eat."

Molly's son smiled and answered, "*Ya.*"

After glancing at Priscilla, Jonathan faced Molly. "How many siblings do you have?"

"I have four sisters and one brother. Do you have any sisters or brothers?"

"*Ya*, I have one of each."

Isaac pulled on her hand and said urgently, "See, *Aenti.*"

"I better take him now to Priscilla. I'll be right back," Molly said.

It was obvious that Priscilla was Molly's sister. They resembled each other a lot with their auburn hair and striking looks. While he watched Priscilla grab the toddler's hand, he wondered, what in the world could Molly want to talk to him about? Was it something she wanted to ask him about the fire? He knew Nicole Spencer had been busy trying to get answers about who could have started the fire. He didn't have anything to add.

When Molly returned, she said, "Let's go outside so no one will overhear us."

Now he was concerned. It had to be something about the fire. Was Molly investigating it herself? She had enough on her shoulders without trying to solve the identity of the arsonist.

He opened the door and held it for Molly. As they walked away from the house, he said, "It's chilly but the sun makes it seem warmer."

"*Ya*, it is a nice day." After she stopped walking, Molly said, "Let's talk here by the creek."

"Your little boy is cute."

"Isaac's always been a good baby." She tucked a lock of hair back inside her prayer covering. "Yesterday, my grandpa found an envelope on the front porch. Did you see anyone put it there?"

He shook his head. "*Nee*. What was in it?"

"Money and an unsigned note. I'm disappointed Robert and Martha Weaver aren't here today. I wanted to show the note to them to see if the handwriting was the same."

"Same as what?"

"There were two other envelopes delivered. One was left at Weaver's Bakery for the food for the men working on the barn. Then someone left a note with money for the lumber. Nicole said it was the same handwriting as the other note that was left with the money for the food. Obviously, I never saw these notes." She gave him a thoughtful expression. "I could see if Samuel or Jacob saw either note but I'll wait. Nicole is coming this evening to see the recent note. She's going to bring the other two so that we can compare the handwriting."

He shrugged. "I know you want to thank the person or persons for the money, but they apparently want to remain anonymous."

She raised her eyebrows. "It's not you, is it?"

He chuckled. "If you saw my bank account, you'd realize it isn't. I just bought a farm."

She leaned against a tree trunk. "Do you think it could be the arsonist who gave me money because he feels guilty that the fire killed Caleb?"

"I guess that could be possible, but it seems doubtful." He thought for a moment but no one came to his mind that would be so generous. "I can't think of anyone who might have given you the money. You might show the note to Caleb's parents. Maybe they will have a clue to the donor."

She frowned. "Rose and Andy aren't here today. I had hoped they would be."

"I wonder if the person is English and doesn't know your father is the bishop. They might not be aware that the Amish have a fund for medical expenses and other emergencies."

"Emergencies like being a widow with a child and one on the way." She murmured. "*Ach*, I see Levi Lantz glancing at us. I'm surprised he stepped outside instead of getting something to eat. Let's hurry and go back to the house. We can go in another door. Otherwise, we'll be detained for too long of a time by our talkative deacon."

Jonathan wondered if Levi was an old boyfriend of Molly's. He'd noticed the deacon had watched Molly closely several times the other day when they worked on building the new barn. Before Levi left the porch, another man opened the back door.

Molly smiled. "My brother Luke is talking to Levi. They will be busy discussing the new buggy Levi wants to buy." Her steps slowed as she turned to stare at him. "I forgot you probably don't know that Luke owns the buggy shop in Fields Corner."

He shook his head. "I didn't know that."

Molly frowned. "It's sad, though, why Levi needs another a new buggy. Five months ago, a car hit their buggy and killed his wife. Levi is a widower now with four children. A relative loaned him a buggy until his new one is finished."

Within minutes, they walked up the steps to the back porch. He and Molly greeted both Luke and Levi as they walked past them on the back porch.

Jonathan couldn't miss the long glance Levi gave Molly. Was he already looking for a new wife? It seemed too soon to him, but sometimes Amish men with children did remarry quickly after losing their wives. Surely, the deacon couldn't be considering Molly already. From what she had told him today, Molly definitely wasn't ready to move on. She had loved her young husband. He'd seen the deep anguish on her face, and she definitely needed more time to grieve.

CHAPTER FIVE

Molly opened the back door and hugged Nicole. "*Danki* for coming this evening. I appreciate you making a trip to see it."

"Are you kidding? I love coming to your house to visit with you."

"And Isaac." Molly smiled at her English friend. Nicole's long blonde hair wasn't pulled back into a ponytail today. She wore a dark denim jacket with a beige blouse and jeans. Her dangling silver earrings reminded her of how Violet used to wear the same type of jewelry. Molly wondered if Violet might someday regret joining their Amish church. She definitely must love Luke to give up so many English things.

"Where is the little guy?"

"My *mamm* took him after our church service, so I could take a nap." Molly remembered how her mother wanted her to go home with them and to rest there. "I have the note on the kitchen counter."

Nicole walked to the counter and picked up the note. Her eyebrows knitted with concentration as she silently read the note. "Wow, someone definitely wants to ease their conscience, or has a generous heart. I have the other notes with me, but the handwriting is definitely the same . . . neat and small."

Now that she knew the same person wrote the note as the other ones, Molly still couldn't imagine who would give her money. "So do you think it could be the arsonist? And he or she feels guilty for setting the fire?"

Nicole glanced again at the note. "It could be, but it's doubtful. And the arsonist is probably male. Ninety per cent of the time, the arsonist is male."

"I can't think of any man or boy who has a grudge against us except for a very small number of English individuals." Molly removed a blue plate from the cupboard. "How about coffee and my cinnamon bread?"

"I love your bread." Nicole gave her a serious look. "I remembered something you said to me recently about how you got this place at a lower price because it was a foreclosure. That got me to thinking how maybe the person was angry that you and Caleb bought it. I doubt this is what happened, but it might be worthwhile to check it out."

Molly unwrapped the loaf of bread and sliced two thick pieces. She carried a cup of coffee and the small plate with bread, placing both on the table in front of Nicole. "I suppose that is a possibility. I'm sure they were unhappy about losing their house and property. From what I heard, they didn't keep up with the remaining house payments or real estate taxes."

Nicole broke off a piece of bread. "Do you know their names?"

Molly shook her head. "No, I don't. Sorry. They kept to themselves."

"It's okay. I can find out." Nicole sipped her coffee.

Opening the refrigerator, Molly took out a pitcher of milk. After pouring a glass of milk for herself, she carried it to the table to join Nicole. "I wish I could be more help with your investigation. I never heard anything negative about the former owners."

"That's true. I doubt it is them, but it will be good to eliminate them for sure. Jonathan mentioned to me recently about a barn fire in Kenton, and how it was caused by an Amish man who had been excommunicated for some time. I asked your father if there could be someone in your community who felt resentment for being barred from his Amish family. He couldn't think of anyone." Nicole took another bite of bread. "You'll have to give me the recipe for this cinnamon bread as long as it doesn't require lots of time. It's delicious."

"It's easy to make."

Nicole laughed. "When you say easy to make, I'm wondering what that means. I know the Amish have a wonderful friendship bread recipe that uses a starter, and the process takes seventeen days."

"This recipe won't take days because you don't need the starter for it."

"That's good. I should be able to make it." Nicole wiped her mouth with a napkin. "I just thought of something. If I attended an Amish church service with you, I could talk to people afterwards. Maybe there would be something said that could help the investigation. What do you think?"

Should she warned Nicole how long their services lasted? "Sure, you can go but I don't know if you will learn anything. Just so you know, the church service lasts around three hours. We begin with thirty minutes of singing and have two sermons that are given by different ministers. We sit on hard, wooden-backed benches during the service."

"The Protestant church I go to has pews, but I can see why you use benches. They are lighter to move since you rotate where your church is held."

"They also move the benches to use for the noon meal. Luke went to church once with Violet in Fields Corner. She wanted him to see the religion she practiced."

Nicole sipped her coffee. "Violet definitely made major changes when she became Amish. She grew up so differently so it had to be difficult to adapt."

Molly nodded. "Although we have outsiders to try to convert to our way of life, it's rare for them to remain. Few Englishers are able to give up computers, telephones, and electricity. I think it's helped that Violet's mother, Carrie, was raised in an Amish home. While growing up, Violet enjoyed visiting her Amish relatives a lot."

Nicole smiled. "What about clothing? Has Violet had a problem switching to wearing plain dresses all the time?"

Molly laughed. "The straight pins gave her trouble. Violet stuck herself a few times. In lieu of buttons and zippers, we use straight pins."

"I didn't know that." Nicole gave her puzzled glance. "Why do you have to use pins?"

"We can use hook-and-eye-closures. I don't because I'm adept at using pins, so I skip sewing the hooks and eyes in my clothing. The ban on buttons goes back to the days in Paris when they were a fashion rage and a way to display wealth. The buttons were costly and showy, so the church leaders made a ban on buttons." Molly smiled. "Violet decided to go with the hooks and eyes."

"I can see advantages to wearing plain clothing. You don't have to spend time worrying about what to wear, and you won't see anyone at an Amish event dressed inappropriately."

"*Ya*, that's right. Our clothing goes along with our belief that we should be separate from the surrounding world. 'And be not conformed to this world' is from chapter twelve in the book of Romans. It's preached a lot to us from the time we are small."

"You said your mom took Isaac so you could a nap. Aren't you sleeping any better?"

"No. It has been rough. I wake up several times a night." Her throat closed around a knot of emotion. She didn't want to start crying because she might lose it altogether.

Nicole reached her hand across the table and grasped her hand. "Hey, how about you spend the night at my apartment some night. It'll be a break for you and get you away from here. Maybe you will be able to sleep. I'll borrow a car seat from a friend, and pick you and Isaac up."

Molly was touched that Nicole invited her to spend time at her place. At first, it seemed crazy to agree to go to an English woman's place, but it would break the monotony of being in this house without Caleb. At her age, she shouldn't be worried what her *daed* thought, but it was hard not to, especially with him being the bishop in their church district. She knew that he might not approve of her going to Nicole's apartment. Although he had mellowed in many ways about Englishers, Molly wasn't sure he would like her staying overnight at Nicole's.

In the past, he wouldn't allow any of the girls in the family to work in Fields Corner because he hadn't wanted them to be tempted by the worldly non-Amish customers. Many English tourists shopped at the stores. He even said no to them working in the bakery, which was owned by the Weavers. It seemed to her that should be fine since the Weaver family were also Amish, but her strict father felt too many English ate there. Her sister Beth had kidded how she got married young, so that she could be free to work in the florist's shop in town. Finally, their sister, Priscilla, got permission from their father to work in the quilting and fabric store in Fields Corner. Maybe Violet influenced her father to realize it was okay to socialize with non-Amish people. Although he'd been opposed to Luke dating the daughter of a popular U.S. senator, he'd changed his mind when Violet had saved Luke's life.

Molly said, "That's kind of you. I'll think about it. Before Grandpa and Grandma came to stay with me, I had a bad time at suppertime. It was one of the most difficult parts of my day because I enjoyed cooking a big meal for Caleb, and we liked spending time playing board games or doing a puzzle in the evening. Sometimes we would sit on the front porch after Isaac went to bed. We'd enjoy a cup of hot chocolate if chilly outside or a cold drink during the summer time." Tears filled her eyes.

"I can't imagine what you're going through. I'm so sorry Caleb died." Nicole paused for a moment, then asked, "Is there a group in your church you could attend that might help you?"

Molly removed a napkin from the holder on the table. Wiping her eyes, she said, "There are several of us who like to meet every other week. We might quilt, bake, or play board games, but I haven't felt like attending since the fire. I almost went last week when Ella Hershberger invited me to a quilting bee. I took the buggy to go to her house, but before I got there, I turned around and came back home. I knew my *freinden* would look at me with pity in their eyes."

A thoughtful expression crossed Nicole's face. "You might attend a support group in town that meets. If you're interested, I'll call the social worker, Debbie Martin . . . she's in charge of the group. I can pick you up and take you. I think it might be helpful. Both Amish and non-Amish go to the sessions to talk about loved ones who they have lost. I've only heard good things about it."

"I remember Violet invited my sister Beth to a support group for parents who have experienced the death of a baby, so she could share her feelings. I don't think I ever told you that Beth and Henry's firstborn, Nora Marie, was a stillborn." Molly remembered all the pain they had experienced at the loss of Nora Marie.

"That is sad. I'm so sorry."

"I and the whole family got to hold Nora Marie after she was born. She was such a precious baby with long eyelashes. She looked like an angel." Molly paused for a moment, picturing her niece and wishing she'd lived. "Beth went through a lot more after Nora Marie's death. Do you remember hearing about a baby being kidnapped? It happened last October. It was Beth's and Henry's baby."

"I wasn't living in Fields Corner then, but I remember hearing something about a baby being kidnapped at an Amish school fundraiser. That must have been terrifying when it was your niece. I was relieved when they found the baby. I was afraid it wouldn't end well."

"It didn't end well for Beth and Henry because they had adopted the baby from Chloe Parrish. Beth and Chloe had met at the doctor's office during a prenatal visit. They became friends, and Chloe decided not to keep her baby. Her parents and ex-boyfriend weren't supportive. She was single and a teenager. Soon after giving birth, Chloe gave baby Emma to Beth and Henry to raise. It was soon after that Nora died. After their baby was found, Chloe wanted Emma back. She regretted giving her daughter away. No adoption papers had ever been signed. Beth and Henry weren't happy about giving Emma to Chloe but they did."

Nicole frowned. "Your sister has really been through a lot of pain."

"*Ya*, she definitely has. During this difficult time, Beth learned she was expecting twins. We're praying the twins will be fine."

"I'll pray for Beth's pregnancy. I hope the twins will be healthy."

Molly took a drink of her milk and thought more about what Nicole had said about the group of people meeting to share their losses. Although Beth hadn't gone to any group for grief-stricken parents, maybe it would help her to attend a group. She couldn't go on like she had been. Isaac and her unborn child deserved the best life she could give them. Bouts of crying spells and feeling sad were not healthy for her *kinner*. "Nicole, call Debbie. I want to go

to a meeting, but would you stay with me? If I feel too uncomfortable, I might want to leave the session early."

* * *

While Perry checked his smartphone for messages, he sat in his
favorite recliner. It was such a comfortable chair that he occasionally fell asleep in it. At age thirty-three, he felt that shouldn't
happen. He was still a young man and should be able to stay
awake while sitting and watching TV. Stacie and Mia sat on the
loveseat together. As his sister read aloud a book to Mia, he
glanced at them frequently. It was nice to see Stacie appearing
more relaxed and happier than she had been for a long time.
While reading to Mia, Stacie changed her voice for the different
characters in the story. She hadn't done that since before Caleb
died. He was relieved to see her more like her old self, but wondered then if maybe she hadn't started the fire.

If she hadn't been the one to cause the tragedy, why had Stacie
said sadly, "That wasn't supposed to happen". He'd heard her
mumble this sentence after they learned Caleb had died. That was
the final clue for him with the other evidence he already knew that
pointed to his sister. Perry realized then Stacie could be the arsonist.

Just thinking about Caleb's death and realizing Stacie could be
responsible made his chest hurt. He disliked having the negative
feelings about his sister, but until the arsonist was caught, he
would continue to suspect that Stacie was guilty.

Glancing at the wall clock, he saw it was eight-fifteen. After he tucked Mia in bed and heard her prayers, maybe he should talk to Stacie. He could casually mention that he hoped the arsonist would be caught soon, so that the widow and family would have some closure. If she had started the fire, Stacie might open up and tell him. *Not a good idea*, he suddenly thought. *What if she confesses, I'll have to tell her to go to the police and tell them what she did.*

When his cell phone rang, he didn't recognize the number. He answered it anyhow.

"Hello, I'm Holly Haney, Dr. Haney's daughter. Is this Dr. Knupp?"

"Yes, it is."

"My father is in the hospital. He's going to have a triple bypass surgery."

"I'm sorry to hear he needs heart surgery."

"Thank you. I'm not sure how long he'll be unable to work. His backup doctor is out of state right now spending time with a new grandchild. You're the closest veterinarian for large animals to us. I remember meeting you at a horse auction. And my dad heard from some of the Amish farmers that you helped with the barn raising for the bishop's daughter." She gave a nervous laugh. "Would you be able to take over my father's practice for the next couple of weeks? Just until the other veterinarian returns."

Perry thought for a moment if he should do this extra work. He didn't want to miss too much time with Mia, but it would be an opportunity to replace some of the money he gave to Molly Ebersol. He was financially stable, but he hoped that Stacie would decide to return to college. After she had attended a couple of years, Stacie had dropped out because of Caleb. All her free time, she wanted to spend with him. If Stacie did decide to go back to college, he definitely wanted to pay her tuition. Of course, he needed to check with Stacie first to see if she could stay with Mia if he should be away for this extra job. "I need to think about it and talk to my sister. She helps me out with watching my young daughter. I can let you know tomorrow."

After the young woman thanked him, they ended the call. Staring at his phone's screen, he sighed. Much of Dr. Haney's medical business came from the Amish farmers. Without a doubt, he might encounter Caleb's friends and family. He was glad he'd told Holly that he needed to talk to his sister before committing. It might not be a good idea to cover for Dr. Haney.

CHAPTER SIX

Amos studied his eldest daughter's face, noticing the sadness in her eyes. He knew it was too soon to see Molly happier, but he had been glad to see her smile a couple of times at the barn raising. He couldn't imagine what Molly must be experiencing, and having to give birth without Caleb would be heartbreaking. The couple had been elated to be expecting another *boppli* so soon after Isaac. They hoped to have a large Amish family. His son-in-law shouldn't have gone into a barn that was engulfed with raging flames.

After his friend, David Hershberger's *fraa*, Irene, died unexpectedly from a heart attack, Amos realized how hard it would be for him to lose Lillian. He hoped that God would bless them with many more years together. His love for Lillian grew from a young man's sweet and romantic love to a deeper relationship. Even though he was the bishop for their church district, Amos appreciated Lillian's spiritual guidance during times of decision making for their Plain people. It was always helpful to get her feedback when he needed another perspective. Sometimes they prayed together about a problem needing to be resolved for their church members. True, he discussed and prayed with the ministers about any needed changes that might be important for their district, but bouncing off various ideas with Lillian kept things lively and interesting between them.

Although the Englishers thought the Amish never changed through the years, it was untrue. Sure, they still drove buggies, wore their simple clothing, and didn't use electricity. However, as districts grew and divided into new ones, the *Ordnung* made changes to adapt as new technologies and issues came up.

After a delicious supper of his favorite meal of meatloaf and mashed potatoes, he absentmindedly sipped his coffee while considering what to say to ease Molly's pain. Telling her that in time things would get better might not help at all. Her loss was still fresh and burning a hole in her heart and spirit. In the past, he had the words to express to grieving widows, but now found himself speechless for his young daughter. Before he got a chance to bring up anything, Molly cleared her throat. When he saw her winding her *kapp* string around her finger, Amos realized she wanted to ask him something of importance. Since she'd been a young girl, he had noticed Molly with this nervous habit of fiddling with her *kapp* strings.

"*Daed*, I want to get a cell phone so when I'm in labor I can call Violet right away. I had a short labor with Isaac so I am expecting it might go even faster this time. I don't need a fancy smartphone like Violet's . . . just a simple one for emergencies. Or if something happens with Isaac and I need to call quickly, I'd like to have a phone close by."

As Lillian picked up his empty plate, she said, "You have a phone in the shanty you share with your neighbors. A better idea is for you to move home with us for the last few months of your pregnancy. I don't like you living in the house alone. *Mamm* and *Daed* need to leave this month to go home. Reuben didn't mind taking care of the livestock while they were in Florida, but he has his own fields to get planted."

Molly stopped twisting her *kapp's* string and frowned. "I know *Mammi and Daadi* are leaving in a couple of weeks. They told me Uncle Reuben wrote them, and asked when to expect them home. I don't want to move back here to have the baby." She gave a weak smile. "You both will try to convince me to stay and sell my house."

Lillian shook her head. "I don't think you should make any decision about selling your house right now."

Amos realized Molly's phone shanty was a bit far with sharing it with her neighbors. He'd been surprised that Caleb hadn't gotten a phone for them in the barn or on their property somewhere, especially when he started his horse business. "How about you have a phone installed in your barn? That way you'll have one close."

"That's a good suggestion, *Daed*, but I want a cell phone when I drive the buggy."

After Lillian finished stacking the dishes by the sink, she turned around to stare at Molly. "We don't have a cell phone and have never needed one while traveling in our buggy."

"I'm glad you haven't needed a cell phone, *Mamm*, but I'm thankful Judith had one when she found her brothers in the cold freezing water in Ruth's pond. Remember, they fell through the ice. It was a blessing that Judith could hurry and call 911 for help."

Lillian nodded. "It was. But remember that Judith was in her *rumspringa* at the time when she had a cell phone."

"Unfortunately, some of our teenagers are using cell phones. You know that I don't like it and I have cautioned the parents to make sure they are not getting on the internet. There is too much bad stuff on the internet. Having access to it might make our youth stray to worldly things. I know the smartphones are like small computers." Amos felt he should mention something about Violet having a smartphone. "By the way, you mentioned Violet's fancy phone. She needs it for her job as a midwife. Otherwise, I never would've approved it for her. I trust her to only use it for emergencies."

Molly's blue eyes widened. "Also Violet does have some English patients wanting home births. Violet told me they call her frequently, and that's not really for emergencies. But Dr. Cunningham is happy their patients contact her instead of him all the time."

Amos decided to steer the conversation in another direction. He smiled at Molly. "Your *mamm* and I are looking forward to holding your newborn and Beth's twin babies when they all arrive."

Molly reached across the table for his hand, giving it a quick squeeze. "I'm glad you understood about me wanting a website to sell my quilts. With my business, having a phone in the house will make it handy to check with Nicole about any online sales. I don't think it will be easy to go to the phone in the barn or to the one in the shared shanty with Isaac and my new baby."

Amos said, "Has Nicole . . ." and he abruptly stopped and continued with, "Is Chloe still picking you and Isaac up?" After he started mentioning Nicole's name, he realized it wasn't a good time to ask if there was any new information about the fire tragedy. Although he wasn't sure about Molly getting a cell phone, it was good to talk about something other than the fire.

"Chloe is picking us up at seven o'clock." Molly stood and went to the counter by Lillian. "*Mamm*, I'll wash the dishes. You cooked and I'll clean up."

"I'd love to see Emma. I hope Chloe isn't in a rush to get back to Cincinnati." Lillian handed the dishrag to Molly. "*Danki* for helping with the dishes."

"I'd like to see Emma too." Amos knew Chloe and Emma were visiting with Beth and Henry. He was glad that their friendship had regained its closeness. It had been rough at first with Chloe deciding she wanted her baby back. From the beginning, he had been afraid Chloe would change her mind about having Beth and Henry raise her baby. If it hadn't happened after the kidnapping, he had been certain that it might have months later. As hard as it was on Beth and Henry to lose Emma, it would have been even more difficult if they had had her longer than the two months.

Molly squirted soap into the sink and turned on the faucet. "Beth and Henry were disappointed that Chloe isn't marrying Tony until November. She'll be twenty then. Also, she is taking college courses in Cincinnati. She plans to become a science teacher. At least, Chloe comes here a lot to see Tony and always makes a point to see Beth."

"And Chloe always brings Emma with her. She is such an adorable baby." Lillian squeezed Molly's shoulder. "I'll go to the living room and check on another adorable child. I'm sure Sadie is having fun playing with Isaac."

After Lillian left the kitchen, Molly stared at the window. "We have company."

Amos glanced at the wall clock. "It's only six o'clock. I'm surprised Chloe came early. Usually she and Beth find a lot to talk about."

Molly moaned as she leaned closer to the window. "It's not Chloe. I can't believe he had to visit while I'm here. It's Levi Lantz."

After opening the kitchen door, Amos watched Levi hitch his horse to the post. As he drew closer to the porch, Amos said, "Good evening, Levi."

"I'm sorry if I'm disturbing your supper, but my mother is with the girls. She's anxious to get back home."

"We've finished eating. Come on in." Amos patted the shorter man on his shoulder.

As Levi stepped into the room, he said, "Molly, it's *gut* to see you."

Molly nodded. "Would you like a cup of *kaffi?*"

"*Nee,* I'm fine, but *danki.*"

Amos chuckled as he pulled a chair out for Levi. "I didn't forget a meeting, I hope."

Levi shook his head before sitting. "I thought I should bring something to your attention about Jonathan Mast."

Amos noticed Molly stopped washing dishes. She turned to stare at Levi, but she wasn't the only one wondering what Levi had to say about their new friend. Having a feeling, it could be a long discussion, Amos decided to get more coffee to drink. Levi wouldn't have driven to their house for just a minor issue. After carrying his cup to the stove, he turned to Levi and asked, "Are you sure you don't want a cup of *kaffi*? I'm going to refill my cup."

Levi removed his straw hat. "*Nee*. I drank a few cups already."

Amos returned to the table with his steaming cup of coffee, and watched Levi turning his hat and fingering the brim of it. "What do you want to tell me about Jonathan?"

Molly dried her hands on a kitchen towel. "*Ya*, what is it? Jonathan has been a big help to my family and me. It was *wunderbaar gut* how he just moved to our district, and instantly helped with the barn raising."

"It is nice he did that, except I think he had a reason for being so helpful. He wants to get on our good side, so that we will not complain about him being a firefighter with the English firefighters. We can't allow him to be in our church district if he wants to continue being a fireman."

Molly frowned. "I don't think it's up to us. I think it's great he volunteers for the Fields Corner fire department. Why would you want him to give it up?"

Amos sipped his cup of coffee. "I think Levi is questioning it because we have never had a church member join the fire department. I don't see a problem with Jonathan being part of the fire company, but I will pray about it."

"Are you forgetting that we are to remain separate from the world?" Levi said in a stern voice. "Jonathan shouldn't be involved with the other volunteers. Not only is he spending time with the

English men, but also I noticed that he carries a cell phone. I understand why he needs it, so he can be alerted when there is a fire. The thing is it's another way he's being tied to the world."

Molly dried her hands on a kitchen towel and crossed her arms in front of her chest. "Maybe we should have more Amish firefighters. We have Amish businesses in town, we participate in benefit auctions with the Englishers, we do blood donations, and we commit to other causes. I'm glad you brought this up, Levi, because I realize we should have more men from our district to represent the Amish."

From Levi's alarmed expression, Amos knew he had his own fire to put out before Molly said more. "I'll talk to the ministers this week about this issue."

"What about speaking to Jonathan?" Levi asked. "You need to tell him about our concerns. You should ask him if he is baptized. Maybe he has put it off because of being a firefighter. Maybe where he came from, they didn't allow the Amish to be firefighters."

"I'll talk to Jonathan about his involvement." He held up his hand. "Just to learn more about it, not to tell him to quit."

Molly grinned. "I'll warn him that the bishop is coming to speak to him. He'll be at my house tomorrow to work in the fields."

Levi arched his one eyebrow. "I know Jonathan is helping your grandfather with the planting, but don't forget I offered to help too. I'm *froh* to help in any way I can."

"*Danki*, Levi. That's kind of you."

Amos and Levi continued their conversation for a few minutes, but not about firefighters. They spoke about the financial aid fund and various families in their district who needed assistance with medical bills. Out of the corner of his eye, Amos saw Molly roll her eyes. He knew she didn't want money from their fund. She was an independent woman and wanted to cover her expenses herself. If she hadn't received money from the anonymous donor, Molly wouldn't have had a choice. He knew Caleb had spent most of their savings on his horse business.

After Levi said his goodbye and left, Amos wondered if the deacon was worried about Molly eventually becoming interested in Jonathan. Was he only worried about keeping Jonathan separate from the English men? Or was there more to his visit and Levi wanted to find something wrong with Jonathan? After more time passed, Amos guessed that Levi wanted to ask Molly to marry him. He'd seen him glancing at her frequently at church yesterday and before that at the barn raising. Obviously, he needed a wife to help raise his four daughters. Although his mother helped with the care of the young girls now, she wouldn't want to continue doing it for years. Her younger children and husband needed her too.

I don't think Molly will be taking up Levi's offer of help anytime soon. She seems happy with Jonathan helping. I'm a little surprised because Jonathan stopped her from going into the barn to try to save Caleb. Or maybe she appreciates now that the young firefighter tried to save her husband.

He exhaled a deep breath. *So sad that Caleb died. Will we ever learn who started the fire?*

CHAPTER SEVEN

Jonathan scooped a good amount of potato salad onto his plate. The men had just finished planting corn in the fields for Molly. It had felt great being in the sunshine while working in the fields and breathing in the warm spring air. In the beginning when Jonathan had showed up to help plow the fields, he had declined her offers to eat with them for the midday meal and for supper. Then he decided it was rude of him not to accept Molly's meal offers.

He'd enjoyed being with Molly and her family, especially since his parents and older brother had moved to Wisconsin. His sister, Clara, and her second husband lived in Michigan so he was the only one in his family left in Ohio. It was definitely nicer eating at Molly's house instead of being alone in his small house trailer. He enjoyed working with Ray and both Mary Sue and Molly were excellent cooks. If he wanted to be totally honest with himself, it wasn't just being with a family again that was a blessing, but seeing Molly daily warmed his heart in a way he had never experienced. Sure, he had dated some, but none of the young women had been right for him.

Ray bowed his head and closed his eyes as a signal to the others that it was time to pray over the food. When he was finished, Ray cleared his throat to let them know the prayer was done.

"Molly, where is everyone? Are my other grandchildren afraid there won't be enough food for them?" Ray teased. "I thought Luke and your sisters were joining us for supper." Glancing at Jonathan, he said, "I don't think we eat that much, do you?"

"We don't. Maybe it's our company they don't like," Jonathan, teased back at his friend. While working with Molly's grandfather, Jonathan had learned how much Ray liked to kid everyone. He made farming more fun with his keen sense of humor.

Ray grinned. "Hey, speak for yourself, Jonathan. I'm a charming old man, ain't that right, Molly?"

After Molly put a bib on Isaac, she rolled her lovely blue eyes at her grandfather. "*Ya*, you're such a charmer."

Jonathan glanced at Molly's blue dress, and realized she must like that color. She frequently wore different shades of blue dresses except when she went to church. Then she wore black which was expected of a widow. After his brother-in-law had passed, Clara had worn black to church for a year. When Clara stayed home, she never wore black while grieving. It must be the mourning custom here, too, Jonathan thought.

She placed a small plate of food on Isaac's high chair tray. "Don't worry. Luke and Violet are coming for dessert later. Anna will be stopping in too. She's assisting the new veterinarian with a sick horse at our neighbor's place."

"What new veterinarian?" Ray asked.

Jonathan sipped his iced tea. Although it was only April, the weather had spiked at eighty degrees and he thought the iced tea was a *gut* choice to serve. Molly made it just the way he liked his tea—sweet but not as much sugar as his mother's tea. His brother, Thomas, liked it extremely sweet and his mother had always gone out of her way to please her favorite son.

Molly took a chair next to Isaac's high chair, sitting across from Jonathan. "Scott Haney had a heart attack and the doctor who would usually take his calls is out of the state. I heard from Anna that Holly Haney called Perry Knupp. He lives in Masonville, so it's a bit of a commute for him."

Jonathan nodded. "I remember him. He helped us with the barn raising."

"He seemed nervous but was nice." Ray jabbed a potato with his fork. "I suppose he had never been around so many Amish at once."

Molly handed Isaac his cup of milk, and then she turned to glance at Ray. "He shouldn't have been nervous. He's gone to horse auctions where there have been Amish and non-Amish at them."

"He did seem a little uncomfortable." As Jonathan held his sandwich in his hand, he paused for a moment. "Maybe Knupp had never helped before at a barn raising."

Molly bit her lower lip. "I just remembered something. I went with Caleb to an auction about a year ago. While we were eating lunch, Caleb saw Knupp and said that he'd met him at another horse auction. Caleb left to talk to Knupp about a horse he wanted to buy. I didn't go with him and I finished eating. I noticed both men seemed agitated about something. When we left the auction, Caleb wasn't himself. I asked him what they talked about, and Caleb said that it was just a disagreement about a horse."

Watching Molly bite her bottom lip, Jonathan thought how she had the prettiest lips. He wondered what it would be like to kiss her. *What is wrong with me? I shouldn't think this way about her. She just lost her husband. She's still grieving deeply for him.*

"I guess that makes sense he'd come to help with building the barn because he knew Caleb," Ray said.

"Knupp never talked to me when he came here to help, but I wasn't outside much. Several of the women and *Mamm* took care of the food outside. Everyone was busy working on the barn except when they took time to eat." A puzzled expression crossed Molly's face. "I wonder if I should mention this to Nicole or to the sheriff. They asked me if anyone appeared to have a grudge against Caleb, but it doesn't seem likely that a veterinarian would torch our barn. Knupp wouldn't want to kill any animals."

"You should tell Nicole, but I agree that it's doubtful he had anything to do with the fire." Mary Sue frowned. "Maybe Anna shouldn't be this man's assistant."

"I wish Caleb had confided in me about the argument, but maybe it wasn't a big deal. I'll tell Nicole, but I doubt it is important."

Jonathan swallowed a mouthful of his barbecued beef sandwich. He didn't want to say anything but he wondered why Caleb hadn't explained to Molly what he'd talked about with Knupp. *If I were married to Molly, I wouldn't want to keep secrets from her.*

Mary Sue sipped her iced tea. "I know Anna loves horses and that's why she's been an assistant to Haney, but I'm disappointed she isn't interested doing something more traditional."

"When *Daed* and *Mamm* gave their permission, it was with the understanding that Anna only worked with Haney when he went to Amish farms. I think they hoped she'd realize it wasn't the type of work for a young Amish woman." Molly shrugged. "I was surprised, too, since *Daed* wouldn't allow me or Beth to work in Weaver's Bakery in town. Now he seems more lenient with my younger sisters. Priscilla is allowed to work in the fabric store."

Jonathan felt like mentioning that leniency for the youngest hadn't been true in his family, but he kept quiet. His parents had always expected more of him than they did Thomas, his older brother. Whenever there was an unpleasant farm job to do, he was expected to do it.

Isaac struggled to stand up in his high chair. He said, "Me done."

After Molly wiped her son's little face, Mary Sue moved the tray enough so she could easily lift the little boy out of his chair.

"*Danki, Mammi.* And I appreciated you playing with him while I worked on my quilt this afternoon."

"It's fun spending time with my great-grandson. I just wish we could be here when Beth has her twins." Mary Sue glanced at her husband. "If you and Reuben can get along without me, maybe I'll hire a driver and come back to help Beth with the twins. Mandy can cook for both of you. Reuben's wife hasn't been burning the food like she did when they were first married."

Ray studied his wife. "I'd miss you. I don't like to be apart."

When Jonathan saw the sad expression cross Molly's face, he knew she was thinking how she'd never experience the kind of marriage her grandparents had—the *wunderbaar* blessing of having a lifetime with the love of your life.

Molly cleared her throat. "You might still be here when Beth has her twins. She could go a month early."

Isaac grasped Mary Sue's hand and said, "Let's go."

Mary Sue laughed. "I'm not sure where we're going, but I can't say no to this little one."

After Isaac and his great-grandmother left the kitchen, Ray said, "Jonathan, I have never seen where you live. How about we go this evening? I can help you fix up the trailer before we leave. I just wish I could be here to help you build your house. You have worked hard here to help me get the crops planted."

"I'll be happy to show my house trailer to you, but you don't need to work on it. It's livable and I don't expect to live there long. Some of my friends I work with are going to help me build my house." He glanced at Molly. "I've eaten *appeditlich* meals here and that has been a blessing. It's been great not having to cook and eat by myself."

* * *

As they walked through the single-wide trailer, Ray grinned at Jonathan. "Well, it is cozy, that's for sure. You only have to take a few steps to get to the kitchen from your living room."

"If there is anything you need, let me know." Molly cast a quick glance at him. "Did the trailer come with enough dishes and pans?"

"None of that was left, but I bought just the basic cookware and dishes I have needed," Jonathan answered.

Molly opened a couple of the kitchen cabinet doors, looking at some of the empty shelves. "You have several plates. It looks like you only have a couple of cups and bowls. I have plenty of both so I'll give you a few of mine."

"*Danki.* I usually rinse out the cups right away, but it'll be nice to have more."

"It's nice you have a propane stove," Ray said, "and everything looks decent."

"*Ya*, it's worked out that an Amish young couple lived here, so everything is gas. They even left their gas lamps."

"They didn't stay long. The husband's father died so they went back to live with his mother." Molly raised her eyebrows. "I never thought about it before, but where have you been doing your laundry? I noticed you have a clothesline outside, but I don't see a washing machine in here."

"I've been using the washing machines in town in the laundromat. I bought the metal clothesline, so I wouldn't have to use an electric dryer too. Since it's just a temporary situation I thought it should be okay." Jonathan knew he shouldn't be using electricity, but his other option was to wash his clothes by hand in a tiny sink.

"I could do your laundry at my house."

"*Danki* but it's not any trouble to take it to the laundromat." There was no way he wanted Molly to do his laundry. It would make him too uncomfortable for her to wash his underwear.

Ray touched his shoulder. "My son-in-law is a reasonable man, but don't mention using the laundromat in front of Levi."

Molly stared at him with a concerned expression. "I just thought of something. When I was at my parents' house a few days ago, Levi stopped in to complain to my *daed* about you being a firefighter. We have never had any firemen in our church community, but my father didn't see a problem with it. He told Levi he'd talk to you. Has he said anything to you about volunteering at the fire department?"

Jonathan grinned at Molly. "As a matter of fact, he did yesterday when I was outside planting."

"What? I missed that conversation. Where was I?" Ray asked.

He chuckled. "You said you wanted to take a little break and get a snack. You were gone so long, I thought maybe you decided to take a nap."

Ray gave him an amused glance. "Well, I don't remember being gone that long, but you could be right."

Molly rolled her eyes at both of them. "You two are something . . . like two peas in a pod. Now let's get back to what my *daed* said."

Jonathan was quiet for a moment because Molly had distracted him. She had moved closer to him when she started questioning him. He noticed a few freckles on her face, and her vibrant blue eyes were gorgeous. He could smell her sweet fragrance and wondered if it was from the shampoo she used.

"Hey, Jonathan, did you forget what Amos told you? You aren't a senior citizen like me so you can't use your age for an excuse for forgetting." Then Ray mumbled, "Maybe it's spring fever."

His face felt warm from embarrassment. Shaking his head, he said, "Sorry. He asked me about my previous church, and if I had joined our faith. I told him I had been baptized when I lived in Kenton with my parents. I want to join the Plain community here, and Amos said he'd introduce me to the congregation at the next church day."

Molly's face lit up. "That's *wunderbaar*. I'm glad you are going to join our church."

"Amos also said he doesn't see any problem with me being a firefighter, and realizes it might be good for other men to volunteer. The ministers agree with him."

"I wonder if Caleb had been a volunteer fireman, if that would have made a difference." Sadness laced Molly's voice. "Maybe he wouldn't have rushed into the barn and would've waited for the fire truck. He'd known from fire training that he shouldn't try to save the horses and livestock. An experienced firefighter would have known not to go in."

Jonathan thought how he'd gone in the burning barn to get Caleb. That was one aspect of being a firefighter he hated with a passion. When he and the other firefighters couldn't save someone, it was tragic. Even though that was hard enough, it was even more painful when children died because of a fire.

Ray gave his granddaughter a quick hug. "He might have still reacted the way he did."

"*Ya*, I know." Molly exhaled a deep breath.

"Molly girl, we better get home. Little Isaac likes to see his *mamm* before he goes to bed." Ray glanced at Jonathan. "We owe you so whenever you need help planting your fields, let me know."

Jonathan shrugged. "I don't have that many acres but thanks. I have time to farm this week because I don't have to go to any construction site until next week."

"I enjoyed working in the fields with you, so I'll be here tomorrow," Ray said. "No arguments."

"*Gut nacht,* Jonathan. *Danki* for everything." After speaking, Molly turned from him and walked toward his front door.

"I'll walk out with you. I need to take care of Ginger and feed her."

"It's nice your barn is in good shape," Ray said.

"The barn could use some paint but otherwise it's fine. I'm glad I don't have to spend time building a barn." He opened the door and held it open for Molly and Ray.

Molly grinned at him. "That's funny how we both have horses named for spices. My horse's name is Cinnamon."

He smiled back at her. "Ginger was my brother's horse, but I bought her from him when he moved to Wisconsin. My father and Thomas didn't want to spend money on a truck and driver to haul their horses."

Once outside, Jonathan hated for their visit to end. He'd enjoyed spending time with Molly and Ray.

Molly stopped by the buggy while Ray untethered the horse from the hitching post. She asked, "What do you think of my new horse?"

As he looked at the chestnut horse, Jonathan said, "He's a nice

Saddlebred horse. You did an excellent job selecting him." He was a little disappointed she hadn't asked him for help when she bought the horse.

She smiled. "I had help. Luke and Anna took me to look at horses and told me which ones they thought would be the best for me. It's nice to have a buggy and horse again. Luke gave me a family discount for the buggy plus it's used. I can't afford draft horses right now. I'm glad my *daed* loaned us his to use in the fields." She raised her eyebrows. "I know what you're thinking because you look exactly the way my *daed* did when I told him about buying my buggy and horse."

Jonathan gave a nervous chuckle. "What was I thinking?"

She shrugged, glancing down at her baby bump. "That I shouldn't have gotten a horse and buggy. I don't want to be dependent on others to take me places. My *daed* said he doesn't see how I'll hitch the horse myself, but when it becomes too difficult, my sister Anna plans to stay with me."

"I wasn't thinking about that, but I'll be honest. I was a little hurt you didn't ask me for help to choose your horse, but you and your siblings did an awesome job." He winked at her. "I was also thinking you look very pretty this evening."

Molly look flustered and murmured, "*Danki.*"

After Ray quickly got into the buggy, Jonathan said to Molly, "Let me help you up." As he lifted Molly, a rush of warmth spread throughout his body.

As he waved goodbye to Molly and Ray, he wondered, was it appropriate for him to feel this way about her? She was still grieving for her husband. Would she ever be interested in him?

CHAPTER EIGHT

"Perry, I got all the invoices finished." Stacie glanced away from the computer and smiled at him.

"Thank you. I'm glad I only had to go to three farms for Dr. Haney." The last one was close to Molly Ebersol's farm. Anna King had even invited him to go with her to Molly's house for dessert after they finished doctoring the horse. Of course, he'd refused. He wanted to steer clear of the widow.

"How is it working out for you having the bishop's daughter as your assistant?"

He studied Stacie for a moment, wondering if she was okay with Anna working with him. When the young woman had told him she'd been an assistant to Dr. Haney, he hated to refuse her request to work for him. Stacie looked interested but certainly not upset. "She's been an immense help," he answered. "Anna even confided in me that she wants to be a veterinarian."

Stacie swiveled in her office chair so her whole body faced him. "I admire her goal but I doubt she'll even go to college. The Amish are opposed to higher education. If she does attend college, she probably won't be able to join the Amish church."

Perry wondered if Stacie was thinking of Caleb, and how he'd tried to live in their world. In the end, he'd returned to his Plain community to marry an Amish woman. His love for Stacie hadn't been strong enough for him to stay engaged to his sister. Perry realized there wasn't a trace of bitterness in her voice, but there was something else. Before he could think about it further, their doorbell interrupted his thoughts. "I wonder who that could be."

Quickly, he left his office to go to the front door. After opening it, his chest tightened at the sight of the fire investigator, Nicole Spencer. He recognized her from the barn raising. Was she here to ask Stacie questions? Thank goodness, Mia was at school. He would hate for her to witness them questioning Stacie about the fire.

"Hello, Dr. Knupp. Detective Benning and I are here to ask you a few questions. Could we come in?"

Although he felt relief that they were not here to question Stacie, why were they here to see him? Had they figured out he'd given money to Molly Ebersol? Maybe they assumed he had started the fire, but then he had felt guilty about Caleb's death. "Yes, of course, please come in. We can go to the living room."

Once Miss Spencer and Detective Benning sat on the sofa, he sat in his recliner across from them. Stacie joined them and introduced herself. Nothing he could do about Stacie being in the room with them, but he wished he could. It might be uncomfortable to answer their questions in front of her. If their visit was about the donations, Stacie would be surprised that he'd given money in secret to the widow.

"Dr. Knupp, did you personally know Caleb Ebersol?" Miss Spencer asked.

He gave a direct look at Miss Spencer, a gorgeous blonde with green eyes. "Yes, I did at one time. Caleb was my assistant before he became Amish."

Miss Spencer frowned. "This is the first time I've heard he worked for you. I'm sure Caleb's widow never knew he was your assistant. In fact, Caleb told his wife that you two met at a horse auction. I wonder why Caleb lied to her and felt he needed to keep his job a secret. Did something happen when he worked for you?"

Perry shrugged. "Nothing happened. Caleb was a good assistant. I guess he didn't want his wife to know he'd worked for me . . . since I'm not Amish. I've heard that her bishop father is strict about his children working for Englishers. Maybe that carries over to spouses."

He felt like he'd handled that question well. He didn't dare to look at Stacie to see her reaction to what he said. It had to be hard for her to be reminded that Caleb left them to become Amish. Not only had Caleb hurt Stacie, but him also. He had valued their friendship and thought of Caleb as a younger brother.

"Molly Ebersol said you and Caleb talked at a horse auction that she went to with her husband. Apparently, the conversation became heated because she noticed you both looked upset. What was the conversation about?" Miss Spencer asked, watching his face closely.

Obviously, Caleb hadn't been man enough to tell Molly about his past engagement, and Stacie's pregnancy. What lie had Caleb told Molly about their conversation? Probably something about horses. "I don't recall. Maybe it was a disagreement about a horse."

Stacie touched his arm. "It was about me, wasn't it? Did he ask about me?"

He nodded. "I'm sorry I should've told you. He asked how you were doing."

"Miss Knupp, did you and Caleb have a relationship other than a business one?" Detective Benning asked.

"We were engaged," Stacie said in a clear voice. "Caleb broke up with me when he decided to become Amish. It was a shock because Caleb had never mentioned being raised Amish. And he had a high school diploma, a driver's license, and had even taken some classes at a community college. Our friends weren't Amish either."

Please, Stacie, don't mention that you offered to join the Amish faith. I hope she won't say anything about the baby, Perry thought. *If only Stacie hadn't been here, the questioning might have ended by now.*

"I'm sorry." Compassion appeared in Miss Spencer's green eyes. "I'm guessing you two met when Caleb was in his *rumspringa*. He must have loved you a lot to consider marrying an Englisher. The majority of Amish children join their parents' faith after experiencing their running around time."

Stacie glanced at Perry. "Caleb proposed after I told him I was pregnant. We were happy and we made plans."

"You must've been very hurt that he didn't marry you then," Miss Spencer said to Stacie in a gentle tone.

"I was devastated. I even told him I'd become Amish. I wanted us to be together." Stacie exhaled a deep breath. "He didn't love me enough. I think he only proposed because I was pregnant."

Detective Benning stared at Perry with a thoughtful expression. "You said that Caleb asked about your sister at the auction. Did you and Caleb argue about the baby during the conversation?"

Perry shook his head. "No, because Stacie had a miscarriage."

"Caleb broke up with me after I lost our baby." Stacie pushed her strawberry-blonde hair away from her face. "It was then he mentioned wanting to join the Amish faith."

"I'm sorry for both of your losses. You've been through a lot," Miss Spencer said to Stacie, then she turned to look at him. "Dr. Knupp, where were you the night of the barn fire?"

He stared back and answered, "I was here at home with my daughter, Mia. I did not torch the barn. I can't believe you'd think I could have anything to do with the fire. Caleb and I were friends when he worked for me. I thought a lot of him. True, he disappointed me that he hadn't been honest with us. I wasn't thrilled with him when he broke up with Stacie, but I'd never set his barn on fire."

Detective Benning asked, "Miss Knupp, where were you when the fire occurred?"

Perry swiftly answered the question. "My sister lives with us. My wife died in an automobile accident, so it's been a blessing to have Stacie here to watch Mia when I get called to go to farms. Mia is only nine years old."

Miss Spencer's eyes narrowed as she stared at him. "You didn't mention your sister when you said you were home with your daughter. Was your sister home with you the night the barn was torched?"

"I'll answer that question because my brother has no knowledge where I was that night." Stacie gave a puzzled glance at Miss Spencer. "I wasn't home until later. It was crazy what I did . . ." Stacie hesitated.

Perry swallowed hard and wondered if his sister actually had committed arson.

Stacie cleared her throat. "I was going to go out with my friend, Charlotte, but on my way there, I changed my mind. I went instead to East Fork State Park. Caleb and I used to go there a lot. Caleb proposed to me at the park. He even gave me an engagement ring. I walked along the short trails. I ended up seeing a couple of friends we used to hang out with. I'll get my cell phone before you leave and I'll give you their phone numbers so that you can call them. Their names are Brittany Young and Will Baxter. I didn't start the fire. I'm sorry for his wife and their son. I hope you'll find the person who started the fire."

Detective Benning wrote the names down on his pad. "We'll follow-up and call your friends."

"Where did Caleb live when he worked for you?" Miss Spencer asked, glancing from Perry to Stacie.

"He lived in an apartment in town with Will," Stacie said. "Caleb met Will when they both attended community college."

"Can either of you think of someone who might have had it in for Caleb?" Miss Spencer tapped her pen against her leg. She wore black pants with a pale pink blouse and a jean jacket.

Perry watched her for a moment, thinking how attractive she was. It was too bad she was the fire investigator for this particular case, because Nicole Spencer was someone he wouldn't mind getting to know. Dating someone hadn't crossed his mind since Kathleen had died.

Stacie shook her head. "I can't. It's so sad this happened."

Well, Perry only had thought of one person who possibly might have started the fire. Thankfully, he'd been wrong to suspect Stacie. He raked his hand through his hair. "I wish I could help you but everyone seemed to like Caleb. I wonder if it was a random act against the Amish. Fortunately, there haven't been other fires to the Amish, so that's probably not it either."

After Stacie gave the phone numbers for Will and Brittany and Caleb's former address, Miss Spencer stood and handed a card to Stacie. "In case, either of you think of anything that might help us find the arsonist, please call me."

Detective Benning thanked them for their time and followed Miss Spencer to the door.

Once Perry closed the door behind Miss Spencer and Detective Benning, he said, "Charlotte called to see if you felt better the night of the fire. I wondered where you had gone."

Stacie gave him a small smile. "I didn't feel like going to a movie and I felt a little down about losing Caleb. I knew Charlotte would lecture me that I needed to move on, so I just said I wasn't feeling well . . . which was true in a way. It was nice being with Will and Brittany. I vented a lot of my feelings. I had never done that before with them. They were also hurt that Caleb never mentioned to them about his upbringing. It was a turning point for me after I released my anger about how Caleb had treated me."

"I'm glad you were able to talk to your friends."

"We sat around their campfire and had hot chocolate and s'mores. It turned out to be the best thing for me to do. I'm sorry if I worried you. I should've told you what I did instead. I didn't think about Charlotte calling. I'm surprised you didn't ask me or mention she called."

He shrugged. "I hated to seem like I was checking up on you." For a second, he thought of telling Stacie how he'd given money to Molly, but how could he? Stacie would ask him why he did, and he would have to explain how he'd suspected her of torching the barn. Now in retrospect, he realized he should have known better. His sister would never do such a horrific crime. She was such a sweetheart and a hard worker in the office. She'd always been a wonderful aunt to Mia.

He wondered if it might be a good time to mention the singles group at their church. She was small, petite like their mother had been. With her strawberry-blonde hair and blue eyes, his sister was pretty.

"Hey, have you ever thought of going to the young singles group at our church? I think you would enjoy it."

Stacie laughed. "Are you trying to get rid of me? I saw you eyeing the investigator. You should ask her out. I have to admit I noticed how cute the detective is. Wow, the department sure has two good-looking people on their force."

He rubbed his chin. "Maybe I should ask Miss Spencer out for coffee or something. I can find out if Detective Benning is dating anyone."

"No, don't you dare. That would be embarrassing." Stacie glanced at their huge wall clock. "It'll soon be time to pick up Mia. How about we get pizza tonight?"

"Sounds good to me."

Giving him a reflective glance, Stacie said, "I do feel like dating again. I was crushed when Caleb broke up with me, but it hurt even more when he lost no time in marrying Molly. Right after he died, I wondered if he had married me and not returned to the Plain life, if he'd still be alive. I think it was a hate crime against the Amish. I mean, what else could it be?"

Chapter Nine

As Molly drove her buggy to Ella's house, she enjoyed the lovely April day. The early spring flowers dotting the countryside were picturesque. The women's quilting group decided to meet only on the weeks when they didn't have church service. Maybe Molly could forget about being a widow and enjoy being with her friends. At least, she'd hear gossip that didn't involve the tragic fire at her place. It would be fun to hear about young people who were starting to date, or to listen to news about friends and family. She definitely needed something else to occupy her mind after what she had just learned about Caleb. Joining women to sew on a quilt was definitely the answer.

The previous day Nicole and Detective Benning had stopped by to see her. Nicole hadn't wanted to leave a personal message on her neighbor's shared answering machine. Molly had been surprised to learn from Nicole and the detective that Caleb had worked for Dr. Knupp. Why hadn't Caleb told her that he'd worked for the veterinarian? Obviously, that had meant Caleb knew enough to take care of their horses without having to call a veterinarian as often. Nicole explained how Caleb had his high school diploma and even attended a community college. The other thing Nicole had mentioned was that she and Detective Benning were sure Knupp hadn't torched the barn.

What else hadn't Caleb told her about his past life? Were there other secrets he'd kept from her? She was crushed he hadn't trusted her enough to tell her whatever he had experienced during his *rumspringa*.

While she hitched Cinnamon to the post outside Ella's house, Molly thought how she could talk more with Nicole on Monday about her meeting with Dr. Knupp. She needed to talk with him to see if there was anything else about Caleb she didn't know. Her English friend had offered to drive her to a prenatal appointment at the doctor's office, so that should be a good time to see if Nicole could drive her sometime to the doctor's house.

If Nicole didn't want to or have the time, maybe Anna could arrange for her to talk to Knupp whenever he was called to see a sick animal. He usually liked Anna to be with him since she knew the Amish families. Some were not crazy about dealing with a new veterinarian, and they felt Dr. Haney knew their ways and respected them.

After entering Ella Hershberger's house, Molly hugged her friend. "I'm glad you didn't give up on me and invited me again to your house."

"It's *gut* to see you again. I didn't get to talk to you much at the last church Sunday."

Molly noticed how pretty Ella looked with her rosy cheeks and brown eyes. It was nice to see her friend happy, and knew she'd had a hard time with her pregnancy. "*Mammi* insisted I visit and quilt with you and the others. She's watching Isaac. I'm glad she and *Daadi* decided to stay another week. Uncle Reuben said it's too wet to plant anyhow. Are you feeling better now?"

"*Ya.* The morning sickness has ended. Thank goodness." Ella tucked a few strands of her black hair under her prayer covering.

"Is your mother watching Elijah?"

Ella shook her head. "Peter took him. They were going to see Samuel at the furniture store." Rolling her brown eyes, she said, "Elijah is definitely a daddy's boy now. He only nurses twice a day. In the afternoon, when he takes his nap, and at bedtime. I suppose it's just as well since I'm pregnant."

Molly hadn't realized Ella still nursed Elijah. "Isaac quit nursing a month ago."

Ella patted her arm. "The other women are here and anxious to see you."

Molly followed Ella into the living room, she was happy to see everyone. She stared for a moment at the quilting frame and loved the beautiful design of the quilt. Molly thought that the double wedding ring pattern must be meant for Judith. She and Jacob were getting married soon. She smiled at Judith.

Judith's blue eyes twinkled with amusement. "I can tell what you're thinking. It's not for me. It's going to be sold to an English woman. She requested this design for her daughter. The money will go to the school fund."

Molly grinned at the young teacher. "You're right. I was thinking it might be for you."

"I did pick the same color of blue that is in the quilt for my wedding dress," Judith said.

She'd chosen the same color for her wedding dress, but Molly didn't need to mention it. "Sky blue is a great choice and will match your eyes."

As several women greeted her, Molly said hello to them. Petite Rachel Weaver looked especially big, but she was short-waisted. *In a short time, I'll look like Rachel. I take after my grandmother's petite frame.* Molly remembered briefly how she looked much bigger than Ella during their last pregnancies.

Another expectant young mother present was Katie Stoltzfus. Molly thought how she and her mother had hoped Luke would become interested in Katie. *How wrong we were to think Violet couldn't be the right woman for Luke. She's perfect for him.*

"We're going to eat after we sew for a couple of hours," Ella said.

"That sounds fine to me. I ate a big breakfast because my grandmother kept putting food on my plate." Although Molly kept telling her grandmother not to give her as much food, she continued to do it.

"That sounds like Mary Sue," Ella said. "I enjoyed visiting with her at the last church service."

Carrie, Violet, and Rachel were on one side of the table. Violet pointed to an empty chair next to her. "I saved a chair for you."

"*Danki.*"

After Molly sat in the spot beside Violet, Ella handed her a threaded needle. "I have extra needles if we need them."

Molly noticed a spool of white thread was already at her spot, and she pulled a thimble out of her bag. Across the table, Molly was *froh* to see her old schoolteacher, Ruth, at the quilting bee. Although it was sad David Hershberger had lost his wife, Irene, to a heart attack, Molly thought it was romantic how he'd fallen in love with Ruth Yoder. She couldn't imagine herself getting married again. Caleb was the only man she could ever love, but men were different. They seemed to eventually get lonely and married again after losing a spouse. Sometimes it was because of necessity. No one wanted young children to be motherless.

Ruth, Katie, and Judith were on the same side of the table with an empty spot that Ella quickly took.

"Judith, who are you having for your wedding attendants?" Molly asked, realizing she should know because her mother taught school with Judith. Maybe her *mamm* had told her, but she'd been absorbed in her loss and hadn't cared to listen closely to some conversations about weddings. *From now on, I need to be a better listener.*

"Do you remember Faith Kauffman?" Judith asked.

Molly nodded. "I remember Faith. She and her family moved away a few years ago."

"I'm *froh* she's back here now. We were good friends in school. Faith's going to be one of my attendants. Our new teaching assistant, Hannah Lehman, will be an attendant too. She was a teacher in another district, but Hannah is looking forward to taking my place next school year. They are both busy sewing their attendant dresses. I decided on light blue for them."

"*Mamm's* happy that Hannah started teaching her class in the afternoons, so she can go to Beth's," Molly said.

Violet nodded. "Beth needs to rest and keep her feet up for several hours a day. It's nice of Lillian to take time off to help with housework and cooking."

"Hannah is living with us until she finds a place of her own. It's been great having her." Rachel grinned at them. "I'm not sure Samuel agrees. He doesn't like two women ganging up on him."

Judith laughed. "Poor Samuel. He has mentioned to Jacob that it's nice for you to have Hannah help you with the housework, but he'll be glad when she finds a place to live."

"Our apartment will be available soon." Violet snipped a thread "Luke and I are going to buy my mom's house. It's been nice living in town and close to the birthing center, but we always planned on it being a temporary home. I'll have my nurse-midwife certification this spring. I might as well be close to my home-birth mothers."

Carrie frowned. "We're giving you the house. Your dad and I don't want you to give us money for it."

Violet glanced at her mom. "Luke and I want to pay for it."

Molly knew her brother well, and he wouldn't like the senator to give the house to them. Before Luke and Violet were engaged, Senator Robinson had asked him many questions about his buggy business. He wondered if Luke could support his daughter with his store. Luke wouldn't want to take handouts from Violet's parents.

"Well, we can discuss it more later." Laughing, Carrie glanced around the quilting frame. "I can see you and Luke can afford to buy it. He has a *wunderbaar gut* business, and I see some of your patients sitting here. Or are you giving them a family discount when they have their babies?"

"*Nee*, Violet better not." Molly shook her head. "Luke already gave me a family discount for my buggy."

With a serious expression on her face, Rachel said to Violet, "I want a family discount. I should get two discounts—one for being your cousin and one for being like a sister to you."

Violet rolled her brown eyes. "See what you started, Mom."

"Oh sure, blame me." With her arm, Carrie bumped Violet in a gesture of gentle teasing.

Laughter exploded around the room as Rachel said, "*Aenti* Carrie and Violet, I was kidding you both. Chill."

Violet giggled. "I never heard you use the word chill. I guess while teaching me more Pennsylvania Dutch words, you're picking up some of my vocabulary."

"I have to say we're blessed to have Violet as our midwife. Ada is great, too, but it'll be nice to just have Violet when I give birth." Ella said to Violet, "I'm glad you'll be certified when I have my baby and no doctor will have to be present."

Ruth looked up from her needle. "I had wanted a home birth, but Dr. Foster wanted me to go to the birthing center. Having Leila in the birthing center turned out great, and David said he liked it too."

"I might go to the birthing center," Rachel said. "I'm undecided."

Katie looked up and stared across the quilting frame at Rachel. "It's nice we have a birthing center and have a choice. Timothy and I are looking forward to having our baby at home if possible."

"I hope I have a choice with this baby," Molly mumbled. She definitely hoped to have the little one at her house, and not have to go to the birthing center or hospital. For one thing, it would cost too much.

"I think we can avoid a roadside delivery this time." Violet grinned at her. After leaning toward the floor for a moment, Violet again faced Molly, waving her smartphone. "Your father definitely wants me to be in close touch with my pregnant patients. You call me immediately when you have the first contraction. Or back pain." Violet glanced at Katie and turned her face toward Rachel. "That goes for you two also. It doesn't matter what time it is."

Molly understood why Violet mentioned back pain. The night before Isaac was born, she had severe back pain. It was probably the start of her labor but she hadn't realized it. She walked around for hours and never woke Caleb to tell him how much her back hurt.

She planned on buying a cell phone, but Molly decided not to mention it. She didn't want to chance going into labor, and have difficulty getting to the phone shanty she shared with the neighbors. It wasn't like she had a husband to stay close to her during the last few weeks of her pregnancy.

"How is Beth doing?" Katie asked. "You mentioned that she has to rest in the afternoons."

"She isn't on bed rest or anything," Violet said. "But we do want her to take it easy and rest every afternoon. We want to reduce the chance of some problems that might occur with a multiple birth. But Beth's doing fine. Henry's mom, Beverly, goes daily in the morning to check to see if she can do anything. And like Molly mentioned, Lillian's been stopping by after school."

"*Mamm's* going to quit teaching this week, so she'll be available more." Molly glanced at Judith. "*Danki* for cleaning up after school so she's been able to leave early."

"I'm happy to do it. Anyhow Hannah stays with me to help. Matthew and Noah sometimes help when they aren't needed elsewhere."

"It probably keeps the twins out of trouble that way." Katie grinned. "I hope Beth doesn't have twin boys."

Carrie smiled broadly at Katie. "Hey, those are my nephews you're talking about."

"They haven't been getting into trouble recently." Ruth laughed. "David and I have them visit my *daed* a lot. He keeps them busy in his cabinet shop. Matthew is also busy with training a new horse for my *daed*."

"The twins have a new interest," Judith said, as she unwound a long strip of thread from a spool. "They want to join the fire department when they are old enough."

"They have been timing everything they ride from the house to the fire department. Matthew said he hoped the scooters would be the fastest. He thought not having to hitch a horse will save time."

While talking about her stepsons, Molly thought how pretty Ruth was. She was a woman of medium height with light brown hair and a warm smile that lit up her whole face. It was funny how much marriage agreed with her. She was around thirty-five when she married David, and Ruth looked younger now than she did before she quit teaching.

Rachel nodded. "Samuel's thinking of joining. He's talked to Jonathan Mast a couple of times about it."

"Jacob wants to learn more about it before he commits," Judith said, then looked at her. "Your mother told me Jonathan helped your grandfather on your farm. Does he have any family or friends around here?"

"Jonathan used to live in Kenton. His parents and his oldest brother and family moved to Wisconsin. Jonathan didn't want to leave Ohio. His sister Clara lives in Michigan with her second husband and children." Molly stopped making tiny stitches to think what else there was to mention about Jonathan. "He lives in a house trailer."

Violet frowned. "We should've have had a work *frolic* and helped Jonathan get settled in his trailer. I remember it being rundown when Abigail and Nathan Hilty lived there. I saw Abigail while she was pregnant."

"Jonathan has it looking okay," Molly said, her head bent over, continuing to make the smallest stitches possible. "He said it's livable and plans on building a house soon. He didn't have enough cups and bowls so I gave him several."

Ella stood. "It's almost noon. I'll get the drinks and food on the table. Then we can take a break for the noon meal."

Molly smiled at Ella. "I can't believe how time flies when we're all quilting together."

"The morning has gone fast." Rachel rubbed her belly. "Baby and I are hungry so I'm glad it's time to eat."

Judith removed her thimble. "You're always hungry, Rachel."

"And I'm not as great at sewing as all of you are." Rachel grinned. "I really came for the food."

Ella put pitchers of ice water on a side table. "Here, I thought you came to see us."

Violet looked at Rachel. "Well, we forgive you for coming for the food since you brought your delicious pies."

"I saw Rachel's butterscotch pie in the refrigerator. I'm surprised Samuel let you get out of the house with it." Katie shook her head, laughing. "That brother of mine could eat a whole pie in one day."

Coming here today was definitely what I needed, Molly thought. *It's nice to listen to the women's chatter. And more fun to quilt with others for a change. I'm glad I changed my mind about going to the grieving group. The social worker, Debbie Martin, seemed nice enough when she visited me, but attending a group with mostly Englishers would be stressful for me. I'd feel like I was on display because I'd probably be the only Amish woman present. Being at a quilting bee with women from my own community is mentally more satisfying and relaxing.*

CHAPTER TEN

On Monday, Molly sat across from Nicole in a restaurant booth by a window. She'd insisted on treating her to lunch after her appointment. Molly enjoyed many things about her new friendship with a non-Amish young woman. Of course, if she mentioned Nicole being young, she'd moan and say she was close to thirty with no prospects of having a boyfriend. Maybe she should comment to Nicole how Ruth married at age thirty-five. It wasn't too late for Nicole to meet the love of her life. *I thought I had met mine when I fell in love with Caleb, but now I wonder what kind of a marriage we had; it wasn't based on honesty.*

Nicole glanced at her laptop screen. "It's great Angela's Restaurant has internet for their customers. I should've realized Weaver's Bakery wouldn't have Wi-Fi."

Molly laughed. "The next time I'll treat you to lunch at Weaver's Bakery. I know you wanted to go there. And I can see why you wouldn't realize there isn't internet at Weaver's. The family does have websites for Katie's catering business and for Samuel's furniture business. They probably don't want to influence

Amish teenagers to go there for the internet during their *rum-springa*."

"Hey, I'm fine. After you told me that Angela sells Amish whoopie pies here, I didn't care at all." Nicole gave an appreciative sigh. "Oh my gosh, I love whoopie pies."

"When you drop me off at home, I have a container of goodies for you and I included whoopie pies." Molly and her grandmother had baked an assortment of cookies that Nicole liked to eat. *With the website that Nicole created, maybe I won't lose my house.* "Don't let me forget to give them to you. I have a pregnancy brain some days."

Grinning, Nicole said, "I won't forget. You realize I'll have to get more running in, but eating your delicious baked goods is always worth the extra calories."

"You don't have an ounce of fat on you. And I wish I had your height." Nicole looked pretty in a pair of gray pants with a black lacy top.

"Well, I was overweight as a child until I got on the track team in junior high school. I love running." Nicole turned the laptop around and moved it next to Molly. "Here is your website. I hope you like it. It's not live yet because I wanted your approval first. I used Molly's Amish Quilts for the site's name, like we talked about."

As Molly poured over the website, she couldn't believe how involved it was with all the page headings. "You spent a lot of time on this. Instead of you treating me to lunch, I should pay for yours."

Nicole protested, "No way. I had fun doing your site. Oh, I added a page about Fields Corner and other Amish businesses. People are so interested in anything Amish and I thought it'd be nice to include facts about the town. If you'd rather, I can delete that page."

"No, I like that you did that. It's a good idea to include other businesses."

"I included Sarah Miller's phone number. I'm glad you asked her if you could use her business address and phone number."

"Ella Hershberger thought of it. She teaches quilting classes at Sarah's fabric store." Molly appreciated Ella's suggestion because she didn't want her personal information listed anywhere on the website.

"I didn't realize how many baby quilts you have until I took the pictures. I think you'll sell those quickly." Nicole smiled. "You're going to do great on selling your quilts. They are all striking. It's interesting how you have both traditional and Amish contemporary designs. And if someone wants you to make a customized quilt, they can contact you by an email form or call Sarah's store. Don't forget I can give you any customer information. I'll continue to be your website go-to girl."

"Well, *Daed* told me I can use the computer at the library if I need to, so I have that as a back-up plan. *Danki* for all your work on the website. It's amazing and is perfect." She grinned at Nicole. "I'm officially a businesswoman now. Sarah said she understood why I'm selling online, but she already sold the two quilts I gave her to sell in her store."

"Let's see, you got the burger and fries," the young server said, as she put a plate in front of Molly.

Molly pushed the laptop toward Nicole, so she could put it away during their lunch.

"And here is your burger and salad." The server glanced at them and asked, "Does everything look okay?"

Nicole said, "It looks delicious. Thank you."

As Molly poured ketchup onto her plate, she murmured, "*Danki.*"

The server smiled. "I'll be back later to see if you need refills or anything."

After both women quietly ate their food for a couple of minutes, Nicole said, "Their hamburgers are really good."

"I should've gotten a salad like you, but I love their steak fries." Molly slowly wiped her mouth with a napkin, remembering the last time she had eaten at Angela's Restaurant. She pointed to a booth with dark red seats in the corner of the room. "Caleb and I ate supper in that booth the night of the fire."

Nicole's green eyes filled with concern. "I'm sorry you're reminded of what happened. I shouldn't have brought you here."

She shook her head, swallowing a mouthful of burger. "I'm happy we came here. It's a good memory for me. You see, we seldom went to a restaurant to eat, but he was happy that someone was going to buy one of his horses. He said that he could afford to take me and Isaac out to eat. I didn't know it at the time, but it was Jonathan who offered to buy the horse."

"I wish you could have more wonderful memories with Caleb." Nicole jabbed her fork into her salad. "Don't forget you're always welcome at my apartment if you feel an urge to get away."

"*Danki*, Nicole." Ever since Nicole had told her that Caleb worked for Dr. Knupp, she wanted to find out everything. It bothered her greatly that he hadn't seen fit to share his past with her. She dipped a fry in a small mound of ketchup. "Right now, I'm confused that Caleb kept things from me. It seems logical that his parents knew Caleb had his high school diploma and he worked for Knupp. Caleb probably lived in Masonville when he was a veterinarian's assistant. But Rose and Andy failed to mention any of these facts to you. When you went back to talk to them, did they explain why they kept information from you?"

"You're right that they knew about his job. They said it didn't seem important to tell me before."

"Did they give you other information about Caleb?"

Nicole shook her head. "No, and both times I've gone to their house, they don't seem to like to answer my questions. In fact, Mr. and Mrs. Ebersol acted uncomfortable. I suppose it's because I'm not Amish. I wish they would grasp I want to find the person responsible for their son's death, and they need to tell me anything that can help my investigation."

Molly sipped her glass of ice water. She wanted to ask Nicole if she could drive her to Dr. Knupp's office sometime. When she'd called Nicole to tell her about remembering seeing Knupp at the auction, she'd said, "I don't know if that information will give us any answers about the arsonist, but the fact that Caleb seemed agitated after talking to the veterinarian makes me think there was some kind of history between them that didn't end well." Maybe there had been a lot more to his business relationship with Caleb. Why had the two men gotten into a heated discussion at the horse auction? "Do you think Caleb owed Knupp money? Maybe that was what they discussed at the horse auction."

"I don't think Caleb owed him any money."

Molly noticed Nicole's frown and knew in her heart that there was something her friend wasn't telling her about Caleb. When she'd tried to question her in the car on the way to see Violet and Dr. Tony for her appointment, Nicole had changed the subject. "I want to talk to Dr. Knupp. I'm sure he can shed some light on what was going on with Caleb. Did he tell you anything about their disagreement that I witnessed?"

Nicole held tightly her glass of iced tea. "It was about Knupp's sister, Stacie. She works for her brother."

"I don't understand. Had she been ill?" Why were they even discussing his sister? Then the reason hit her. Caleb must have dated Stacie while he worked for Knupp. "Caleb dated her. Am I right?"

Nicole sipped her drink and looked uncomfortable.

"It's okay. You can tell me."

"I hate to always be the one to tell you stuff about Caleb's past. And especially here."

"I can handle it. I want to know everything you've learned."

"Yes, you're right that Stacie and Caleb dated. He broke up with her, and told them how he wanted to join the Amish church. Stacie and Knupp were surprised to learn Caleb had been raised Amish. Caleb had a high school diploma and had attended a few classes at a community college. Stacie said he also had a driver's license."

Molly's throat closed around a lump. How had no one in their district known about Caleb's living and working as an Englisher? And she felt stupid for not knowing anything about Caleb's former life. "Caleb didn't share any of what he did before we dated. Obviously he never told me about Stacie either. I wonder if I should meet with her and her brother to see what else I was kept in the dark about."

When Nicole's cell phone rang, Molly saw how relieved she looked to have an interruption from their conversation.

After she pulled the phone out of her purse, Nicole said, "It's Justin. I better take it."

As Nicole talked on her phone, Molly felt a knot forming in her throat, and she swallowed hard. The pain of losing Caleb stayed with her all the time, but now to learn he'd lived a totally different life than she ever knew was hurtful. He should have felt free to confide in her. She loved him with her whole heart.

Nicole slipped her phone back into her purse. "Justin has located the couple who used to live in your house. I'm glad he tracked them down. They live in Cleveland so we will take a road trip there. Justin said he'll pick me up at your house. Is it okay if I leave my car at your place?"

"*Ya*, of course." She wrapped a *kapp* tie around her finger, thinking about the woman Caleb dated. If she had loved someone before Caleb entered her life, she would have told him. "Do you think Stacie could be responsible for Caleb's death?"

Nicole shook her head. "We talked to the couple Stacie was with the night of the fire. They confirmed she was with them the whole night."

"I want to meet Stacie. Maybe there's more I should know about the English Caleb. It might be important if there are other things he failed to tell me. I'll see if Carrie Robinson can take me to meet with her. She's here visiting Violet and Luke. I just saw Carrie at a quilting bee I went to at Ella's. Sorry I'm rambling on about everything."

Nicole took a sip of iced tea, then blew out a heavy breath. "I've been torn about all of this. I haven't wanted to upset you, but I have felt you should know about Caleb's past. There is more."

Molly's chest tightened at a terrible thought. "Oh no. Don't tell me he was married to Stacie."

"They became engaged when Stacie learned she was pregnant. Caleb broke up with her when she had a miscarriage. I'm so sorry. I haven't known what to do. I hated to have to tell you about any of what I've learned about Caleb. I talked to Violet while you got dressed after your appointment. I didn't tell her the details but just that I had learned a few things during my investigation. I explained it might be upsetting to you."

Molly couldn't speak when she tried to absorb the shocking news of how Caleb had treated Stacie. He'd gotten her pregnant when they were not married. Amish couples seldom had to get married due to a pregnancy. They believed premarital sex was a sin. Her parents had always stressed they should remain pure for their spouses. Her father and the ministers quoted Bible verses whenever it was mentioned during any of their sermons.

During *rumspringa* most of the youth remained living at home with their parents. Who had Caleb lived with when he moved away from his parents' home? Had he eventually lived with Stacie? In moving away from his home, Caleb must have adopted many non-Amish ways.

"Did Caleb live with Stacie?"

"He lived with a friend called Will Baxter. Caleb met Will when he attended community college."

Although he'd gotten Stacie pregnant, Molly felt a small amount of relief that he had never lived with the English woman. It would've been even harder to hear he had shared a home and bed with Stacie before they had married. During their courtship, Caleb had treated her with respect, but she was troubled that he must have cared enough for Stacie to have sex with her before marriage. Caleb was not the man she had thought he was.

There was one person she needed to see, so she could make sense out of the intense betrayal she felt.

Chapter Eleven

"*Daed*, I need to talk to you. I'm glad you're here by yourself. I was afraid Anna would be here. I mean it would be okay if she would be, but I'd rather talk to you in private."

When Amos heard Molly's distraught voice, he turned around to look at her. He hoped she hadn't received bad news about her pregnancy. But if she had, she'd probably want to talk to Lillian and not him about it. Or one of her sisters. Well, she wouldn't be driving the buggy herself if she had problems with her pregnancy. He leaned his pitchfork against the stall's railing, watching Molly close the barn door behind her.

"Anna went with Dr. Knupp to Levi's house. Something about a sick cow." He wished Dr. Haney hadn't gotten ill. Knupp seemed to be a fine man, but Haney understood that he shouldn't encourage Anna to continue her education and become a veterinarian. It wasn't the Amish way to enter the English world and attend college. Sometime he needed to share their beliefs with Knupp. He was afraid Haney might not be back anytime soon.

"Oh, *Daed*, you aren't going to believe what I've learned about Caleb's past. I still can't wrap my head around what he did."

He took Molly's arm and led her to a stack of hay. He couldn't imagine what Molly had to say about his son-in-law. What had Caleb done that had upset Molly? "Let's sit here. Just take a deep breath and take your time."

She gave him a weak smile, sitting next to him. "Just like when I was a little girl and I came here to chat with you. You've always been a good listener. I have a lot to tell you."

"Well, you came to the right place. I have plenty of time to hear everything." He patted her arm. "Do you want a bottle of water? I have a cooler in here."

She shook her head. "No, *danki*."

"Was it something he did during his running around time?" Some of their Amish teenagers enjoyed doing non-Amish things before they took their baptism instructions . . . like purchasing a cell phone, smoking cigarettes, drinking alcohol, going to movies in a theatre, and attending baseball games. A few even got their driver's license, bought cars and kept generator-operated elec- tronics in their rooms. The boys more often dressed English than the girls. Even though some of their youth experienced many worldly things, he was happy when a high percentage of them de- cided to take instructions so that they could be baptized. Usually they joined when they decided to marry.

However, it seemed like Molly was too upset about what Caleb did. Had he experimented with drugs? That hadn't been a problem with the youth in their district, but Caleb's parents moved to Fields Corner when they had inherited a farm from an uncle. Caleb hadn't grown up in their community.

She twisted a white *kapp* tie around her finger. "Detective Benning and Nicole stopped on Friday to tell me what they had learned about Caleb from Dr. Knupp. During his *rumspringa*, Caleb worked as an assistant to Dr. Knupp and he had his high school diploma."

Amos stroked his gray beard. "Caleb never spoke a word of his education or job to me. He should've been forthright and mentioned it. I wonder why he didn't when it was during his running around time. He wouldn't have been shunned. I'm sorry he didn't tell you, but I guess he was afraid to because I'm the bishop here. I knew you loved him and I wouldn't have discouraged you from marrying him just because he had gotten his diploma or worked for Knupp. It seems that is something he would've wanted to share."

"Caleb's parents admitted knowing about his past when Nicole went back again to see them. She said that they don't seem to realize how important any detail about his past could break the case."

"I wonder if he didn't mention it to us because of them. I'm not sure why his parents would tell him to keep quiet, though."

"I know why. I can't believe it didn't occur to me earlier today, but I guess I was in shock. They might have been afraid if he told about his past life in Masonville, we'd find out what else he did."

Tears filled Molly's lovely blue eyes that were so like Lillian's. He put his arm around her shoulders and drew her closer to his side. He decided to keep quiet and let her speak whenever she felt like it. He couldn't imagine what else Caleb had done.

Molly cleared her throat. "I could deal with him not telling me about his education, but there is more he never bothered to tell me. When they stopped to see me Friday, Nicole and Detective Benning didn't tell me everything. After my appointment today, Nicole told me that Caleb was engaged to Dr. Knupp's younger sister, Stacie. When she had a miscarriage, Caleb broke up with Stacie, and said that it was because he wanted to join our church. They never had a clue he was raised in an Amish family."

Anger rose inside him. He hated seeing the pain on his eldest daughter's face. How could Caleb have kept his past from Molly? He should have definitely told her about Stacie and the pregnancy. He should have told her before he asked her to marry him. "I'm sorry you found out this way."

"I'll take that bottle of water now."

He stood and walked to the cooler and prayed, *Lord, give me the right words to speak to Molly. She has been through so much with losing Caleb and now she's heard hurtful things about him that she never knew.*

He handed her the bottle and sat again beside her. "I didn't know any of this about Caleb. His great-uncle was Amish, but I never personally knew him. When the district grew too large, it was split. Then Caleb's great-uncle was in the old district. When Rose and Andy inherited his house, they continued worshipping with the others in that district. It wasn't until Caleb married you, they started attending our services."

Molly nodded, unscrewing the bottle cap. "It's not your fault. When I met him at a volleyball game, Caleb seemed like a shy Amish man." She gave a tiny smile at him. "Not too shy, I guess. He asked to take me home that first night. I hesitated because I didn't really know him, but Beth went with me."

Amos wondered if Caleb had talked to his bishop in his previous district about having premarital sex. That was something he should have confessed and asked for forgiveness, but he rather doubted Caleb had told any minister or the bishop. "I know Caleb loved you, but he should have been the one to tell you about what he'd done in his past. He must have been afraid you wouldn't have married him if you knew."

Molly took a drink of water. "I don't understand why this happened to me. I have served God faithfully my whole life. I was a *gut* wife but still God took Caleb from me and left Isaac fatherless. Our unborn child won't know Caleb. All that has broken my heart, but now it seems I am being punished even more. I can't talk to Caleb about any of this because he's dead. I feel crushed with sadness in my heart from Caleb's death, but bitterness at the same time. If he appeared in front of me right now, I'd hug him and then slap his face."

His daughter Molly had always been a strong person with an incredible zest for living. Seeing her eyes filled with pain and hearing the defeated sound in her voice broke his heart. He wished he could take her pain away. "Yes, it is unfair what has happened to you, but if you had never married Caleb, you wouldn't have Isaac. He is a wonderful little boy and a blessing. You have a new baby to look forward to, but at the same time it is difficult when Caleb won't be here."

"That's something else I worry about. How can I take care of two small children? Some widows marry again so that their children have a father again. But I don't know if I can trust anyone and I don't want to be dependent on a man again."

"You have every right to feel this way, but don't close your heart to a future with another man who God might bring into your life. I know you can take care of yourself and your children, but it would be nice for you to have a happy second marriage."

"Please don't mention Levi. I know you're close to him since he's your deacon. I've noticed the dark circles under his eyes, and understand what he's going through with losing a spouse. He has four daughters to raise without his wife at his side. Even though I can relate to his difficult situation, I'm not interested in marrying him. He's stopped by a couple of times to see me. He's made comments that he's concerned how I'm going to hitch Cinnamon to my buggy in my condition when *Daadi* leaves. I told him Anna is going to stay with me."

Amos hadn't been thrilled that Molly bought a horse and a buggy, but he'd known better than to argue with her about it. He knew she hadn't wanted to hire a driver each time she wanted to go to town or other places. Molly had to deal with many situations that a young mother shouldn't have to do on her own. "You have suffered greatly with losing Caleb and have now experienced more disappointments, so of course you feel hurt and that is multiplied because you can't confront Caleb with what you've learned. God is with you and He loves you. Jesus said in John 16:33, 'I have told you all this so that you may have peace in me. Here on earth you will have many trials and sorrows. But take heart, because I have overcome the world.' As you draw closer to God for strength and comfort, your bitter feelings will diminish. You need to stay focused on God and not on your circumstances."

She frowned. "Hopefully, I can keep focused on God, but it's hard not to feel resentment."

"You and Caleb were happy before he died, weren't you?"

"*Ya*, we were," Molly murmured.

"Was Caleb a *gut* husband and father?"

"*Ya*, he was."

"Think about how he loved you and Isaac and forgive him for his past. Once you are able to forgive him, you'll be able to move on with your life and will feel whole again."

"I'm not sure he loved me and Isaac when he entered a burning barn."

"It does seem foolish that he ran into the barn when it was a blazing inferno. Even then, he might have thought how the horses cost a great deal of money. If he lost them, he wouldn't be able to provide for his family. Or the shock was so great that Caleb wasn't thinking at all that he would die. His thought might have been that he had to save the animals from a brutal death."

"I am surprised sometimes that I didn't drop dead myself from grief. The first month I kept Caleb's shirt in our bed on his pillow. Each night I smelled it before I went to sleep. It was the shirt he wore our last evening together."

"I'm here for you whenever you need anything or just to talk."

Molly put her head on his shoulder. "*Danki*, Daed. I wish Caleb would have been the man you are. I don't know now if I want to stay in the house we bought together. It was his idea to buy it."

"Are you thinking of moving in with us? I'm all for it." He knew Mary Sue and Ray planned on going back home in a few days, and he hated to think of Molly living with Isaac alone in the house. Sure, Anna planned to stay with Molly and Isaac, but how could she be much help if she was off working with Dr. Knupp? Anna wouldn't like it, but maybe she should quit her job.

Molly lifted her head. Shrugging, she said, "I don't know what to do. I don't like living there without Caleb, but I can't move back home with two little ones—"

"Of course you can live with us. Your mother and I would love to have you and our grandchildren live with us."

"I'll consider it but I thought of someone who might want to live with me."

"I guess it isn't one of your sisters. Who is it?"

"I thought of Hannah Lehman. She could pay rent and have one of the bedrooms. She's living with Rachel and Samuel right now. Violet did mention renting their apartment to her when they move, but maybe Hannah would rather live with me."

He nodded. "Luke said they want to buy Carrie's house."

"If I decide to stay, I should get chickens. I never replaced the ones we lost. I don't want to get any cows. I can buy milk from Jonathan when he gets his cows."

"I like Jonathan. He's already been a good neighbor to you." Amos considered mentioning more about the firefighter, but the barn landline phone ringing interrupted his thoughts.

After he walked to the wall phone and had the receiver next to his ear, he heard Lillian's excited voice. "What is it?"

"Sharon Maddox is on the way to pick us up to go to the birthing center. Beth is having contractions. I don't think we should take time to pick you up. Do you want Sharon to get you and my parents after she drops us off at the center? I know they will want to be there when the babies are born. They stayed in case she'd deliver the twins early."

"Okay, tell Sharon to go to Molly's. I don't want her to make two more stops. Molly's here so we'll take her buggy back to her house." He wondered if Lillian had remembered that Sadie was in school. Since Lillian had started going to Beth's daily, he tried to be home for his youngest child. "What about Sadie? Could she go to the fabric store after school and stay with Priscilla? Obviously, I won't be here when she gets out of school. When Priscilla is done working at the store, they can go to the birthing center."

"I completely forgot about Sadie with all the excitement here. *Ya*, she could go to the store. Could you call Priscilla?"

"*Ya*, I'll call and tell her to go to the school to get Sadie."

CHAPTER TWELVE

On a warm May day, Jonathan pulled a handkerchief out of his pocket and wiped his sweaty forehead. When he saw a buggy turn into his long driveway, his heart raced. Maybe it was Molly coming to visit him. It was her buggy and new horse. Ever since he and his friends had started building his house, he wanted to share the daily progress with Molly. When her mourning period ended, he wanted to court her. It'd been hard to give her the time she needed. Although he could tell she enjoyed his friendship, he hoped it would develop into something much more.

Disappointment threaded through him when he realized it wasn't Molly. However, regret that it wasn't Molly only lasted a moment when he saw the driver was her grandfather. He always enjoyed Ray's visits. He had a feeling his elderly friend stopped to tell him that they were going home soon. He would miss Ray's companionship.

"Looks like you worked hard today. Where are your friends?" Ray asked as he climbed out of the buggy.

"They left at noon to finish another job. I'm grateful to them for coming here first. Now that the framing of the floors, walls, and roof is done, the inspector needs to come here to verify that everything has been done to code." Jonathan waved his straw hat at the skeleton of his house. "What do you think?"

"Looks good from here. I'd like to take a closer look."

"Sure, I want you to see the inside. I'm glad you stopped by."

"I wanted to see you before we leave tomorrow morning."

Jonathan wasn't surprised at the news because they only stayed longer to see Beth's twins. Ray had been antsy about getting home to farm his land. "I hate to see you leave. I appreciate all the help you've given me. It was nice working with you here and at Molly's. It's hard sometimes not having any of my family around here, but you and Mary Sue have become like family to me."

"It's a shame you don't have any family close by. Mary Sue and I think highly of you. You're a good man, Jonathan. I'm glad we hit it off right away." Ray stroked his white beard. "I feel comfortable asking you to check in on Molly on a regular basis. Sure, Anna is going to live with her, but she's a young girl with all kinds of things pulling her in all directions. I know Anna feels torn between our world and the non-Amish one."

"I'll be happy to visit Molly and make sure she's doing okay."

"I told Mary Sue she could stay. I saw she was torn about leaving Molly and Isaac. And she thought about staying to spend more time with Beth and the twins, but I'm relieved she's going home with me. Those babies are something. Even though they were born a little early, both James and Julia are doing fine. They are two weeks old already."

"That's really something you have two new great-grandchildren." He stuck his handkerchief in his pants pocket. Even though

no demonstration of affection were shown in public places between an Amish couple, he'd seen the sweet affectionate glances
and touches between Ray and Mary Sue at Molly's house.

A thoughtful look came into Ray's eyes. "We've been married
for forty-nine years. The only time we were apart was when Mary
Sue came here to help Lillian with some of her babies."

"I'm not surprised. Mary Sue would want to help Lillian as
much as possible."

"One of the best things you can do in life is to marry the one
right person for you . . . the one God has chosen. Anyhow, I don't
like being apart from Mary Sue. I'm going to be seventy-one on
my next birthday, and Mary Sue is sixty-eight. I hope we have
many years left together, but we don't know what God has
planned for us. Each day is precious and being with my lovely *fraa*
makes it even more so."

"I never would've guessed you're going to be seventy-one. You
certainly don't act like it and work as hard or harder than a much
younger man."

Ray smiled broadly at him. "I see what you're doing. You are
giving me compliments so I'll get back here and work on your
house this summer."

He chuckled. "I can't fool you. Come on and look at the house.
I have a cooler with pop and iced tea if you want anything to
drink."

Ray followed him up the steps into the house. "*Danki* but I'll
pass on the drink. I can't stay too long."

"You already saw the basement so we can skip that."

"I've missed our basement. It's built in the hill like yours. We move to the basement in the summer for sleeping. Molly's upstairs is too hot some nights to sleep well, and her house only has a root cellar."

"Let's go upstairs first."

After Ray saw all four bedrooms, they stopped outside the bathroom. "It's good you will have a bathroom on the second floor."

As they walked through the rooms downstairs, he said, "I enjoyed working here and keeping busy while Mary Sue took care of the house and Isaac. That freed Molly to work on her quilting business."

Jonathan nodded. "I'm glad she's had time to sew. Her business should do well. Nicole already took orders from a few of her friends for quilts."

Ray stopped in the spot that was going to be the kitchen. "Everything looks great and the rooms are huge. It's going to be a big change from your small house trailer to living in this house."

"*Ya*, it'll be nice to live in a farmhouse again." Jonathan felt pleased that Ray liked what he saw.

"In fact, the house is plenty big for a lot of people. Do you have a family stashed away that I don't know about?" He asked with a deadpan glance.

"Very funny. I don't have a family hidden away." He grinned. "*Ach*, I know what you're getting at. I'm not planning on living in my house by myself. I'm hoping God will bless me with a *fraa* and *kinner*."

"Do you have any young woman in mind?"

"*Ya*, I do and I think you have an idea who it might be."

Ray nodded. "I've seen the warm glow on her face when you're around. It's nice to see her look a bit happier when you've been at her house. I've noticed the way you've looked at Molly too. I'm hoping I'm right in thinking you're interested in her."

Jonathan sighed. "I am. I know it's too soon to mention anything to her. When the time is right, I hope she'll be interested in dating me."

"It's sad that Caleb died, but Molly is young. She will sometime want to get married again. It's hard on her with being in the family way. I know it bothers her lot that Caleb will never see this little one. I hate that he wasn't truthful about his past, and Molly learned about it now." Ray removed his hat and fingered the brim. "I love all my grandchildren, but Molly has always been my favorite granddaughter. She hates dishonesty, but has a forgiving nature."

"I don't have any secrets. I never was engaged, and I wasn't even serious about anyone until Molly. I never did much during my running around time except I went to a movie once and a Reds baseball game. I'm sorry Caleb wasn't forthcoming about stuff." Jonathan had been surprised to learn Caleb had been engaged to an Englisher. When Molly told him, he'd hated to see how hurt she was; he'd also felt anger. Why hadn't Caleb told her about Stacie? He had to be afraid she might not marry him, but hadn't Caleb realized it would come out eventually?

Ray put his hat back on. "I'm glad you aren't hiding anything. I didn't expect you were. I know you're pretty busy right now, but sometime you should come visit Mary Sue and me in Berlin."

"I'd like to visit you. I've never been to Berlin. How did Lillian end up living so far away from you?"

"Lillian came to visit my sister-in-law. When she met Amos, she extended her visit. He already had a farm here. Hey, I just remembered that Molly sent a loaf of her cinnamon bread. She said you always wolf it down when she makes it."

"I do love her cinnamon bread. It's moist and *appeditlich*."

* * *

After Ray left, Jonathan went back to his house to put the tools away. As he closed the lid on the toolbox, Jonathan thought how sweet it was of Molly to give him a loaf of bread. *I should go to Fields Corner and buy her something nice. What can I get her?*

Thirty minutes later, he arrived in town. He had eaten a couple slices of bread. Then he took a shower and put clean clothes on before he left his trailer. As he drove through Fields Corner, several people waved to him from their buggies. *It feels great to feel part of the community. Such a nice small town,* Jonathan thought. Sure, sometimes he missed his friends in Kenton, but coming here had been the right thing to do. He was able to buy the kind of property he wanted for a good price. He loved the creek that ran back of his new home. He felt a strong sense of belonging at the fire department. All the men were great and had respect for his contribution as a firefighter. His employer had praised his construction work.

As the buggy moved slowly on the street, he looked at each business, thinking how blessed he was that he had decided to move to Fields Corner. It was an excellent place to put roots down and to raise a family. He glanced at Angela's Restaurant. *I should take Molly there to eat when her mourning period ends. Or maybe she'd rather go to Weaver's Bakery. Geez, I can take her to both places.* Samuel Weaver's store was next to his mother's business. He realized how nice it'd be to buy a few quality made pieces of furniture. Next in his view was the florist shop. While glancing at the florist shop, he knew what he could buy for Molly. Flowers would be a nice gesture to show his appreciation. Of course, he could buy flower seeds and plant them for her, but getting a bouquet of flowers seemed like a better choice.

He pulled into a front spot next to a white car. He stared at the florist shop for a moment. *I could get Molly a lovely vase with the flowers. The florist should have some nice vases.*

While he tethered Ginger to a hitching post, a young English man stopped by him, waving his finger angrily at him. "Do you even see what your stupid horse did?"

Jonathan assumed Ginger must have discharged droppings. When he turned his head to look, nothing was there. "I'm sorry. I don't see anything."

The man pointed to a pile of black potting soil that was by and under his front tire. "What about that pile of manure?"

Jonathan chuckled. "My horse didn't discharge potting soil. Someone must have dropped it when they left the florist's shop."

The man placed his hands on his hips. "I thought Amish were supposed to be honest. That isn't potting soil. Even if it is, there have been other times that your horses have made messes all over the streets."

What should I do, Jonathan wondered. *The man obviously has anger issues and he isn't going to stop yelling at me. I'll apologize just so I can get him to shut up.*

Before he could comment, a young woman with blonde hair came out of the florist shop, carrying a bouquet of flowers.

She walked up to the man, placing her hand on his arm. "Jeff, what's wrong?"

"Nothing. It's not worth talking to this stupid farmer about what his horse did." He glared at Jonathan. "Why don't you Amish go elsewhere to live?"

The woman gave Jonathan an apologetic glance. "I'm sorry. My brother didn't mean that."

Jonathan nodded at her. "It's okay."

Jeff opened the car door for her and glared at him. "I did mean it. I'm sick of all the Amish living here. It wouldn't be as bad if they stayed off our streets. I don't get why they are allowed to park their stupid buggies right next to all the stores."

CHAPTER THIRTEEN

After Nicole came into the kitchen, Molly shut the back door, smiling at her son. "Look who's here to visit us. One of our favorite people."

From his high chair, Isaac lifted his chubby hand and waved.

"He loves to say hi, but his mouth is full of Cheerios."

"Hi, Isaac." Nicole grabbed his hand and kissed it. "I've missed you. Have you been a good boy for your mommy?"

His head went up and down several times.

Nicole smiled. "I guess that is a yes." She turned to look at Molly and set a light blue paper bag on the floor. "I bought Isaac a gift. It's a shape sorter cube with nineteen color shapes. It might keep him busy while you're sewing."

"*Danki*, but you didn't need to do that. You've already done so much for me. Would you like something to eat or a cup of coffee?"

"I had a big breakfast with Justin." Nicole sat on a chair on one side of Isaac. "I have some news. We tracked down the previous owners of your house. Their names are Jane and Don Morton. It's taken more time to locate them, because they have moved several times. After Mr. Morton lost his job due to downsizing, they bought this farm because they decided to live a simple life. They thought it'd be cool to live off the land, but they got in over their heads. They knew little about farming."

Isaac banged his sippy cup against his tray, so Molly took it from him. "Your cup feels empty. Do you want more milk?"

He said, "*Ya.*"

As Molly walked to the refrigerator, she said, "I'm surprised the bank loaned them the money."

"The only reason the bank gave them a loan was because of Mrs. Morton's job as a registered nurse. They gave a low down payment because they wanted to use their savings to buy a small tractor and other farm equipment."

"Why would they buy a farm with seventy acres when they didn't know anything about farming?' Molly didn't wait for Nicole to answer and continued, "They apparently never asked for help because I never heard anything about them. But I was single then and it might have been the time I met Caleb. It seems like all I thought about was him."

"From what they told me, it sounded like they stayed to themselves. I don't think they took time to make friends. After they moved here, Mrs. Morton had a nasty fall while they worked on the farm. She broke several bones and also injured her back. She couldn't work for some time so they didn't have a paycheck coming in."

"That's terrible she got injured and couldn't work." Molly gave the refilled cup to Isaac and poured more Cheerios on his high chair tray. "My growing boy loves to eat."

"He's such a cutie." Nicole stood and walked to the stove. "I think I will take a cup of coffee."

"There's cinnamon bread on the counter. I know you can't be too full for my bread." Molly grinned at Nicole.

"You know me too well." Nicole sliced a piece of bread and put it on a napkin. "Where are your grandparents?"

"They left early this morning to go home." From her chair, Molly leaned closer to Isaac and touched his cheek with her finger. "Isaac and I were spoiled while they were here. Weren't we?"

Nicole frowned. "I'm sorry they have left. Is it okay if I buy you a cell phone? I hate for you to be alone here. Your phone shanty isn't that close for you. And before you object, I know some Amish have cell phones for their businesses."

"Anna is going to stay with me sometimes and probably Priscilla will too."

"That's good."

Molly stood and went to her cupboards. "I bought a cheap phone." She opened a drawer, lifted kitchen towels, and removed a phone. "I keep it hidden except at night, and then I put it on my nightstand. I bought a phone card for the minutes."

"I'm glad you bought one. Before I leave, give me your number. I promise I won't use it often, so that you don't go through your phone minutes too quickly."

"I decided if something should happen to Isaac, I might need to call someone right away. Or I might go into labor and give birth fast again." Molly sighed, leaning against the kitchen counter. "Giving birth on the side of the road isn't something I want to have happen again."

Nicole's green eyes widened. "I couldn't believe that when you told me how Isaac was born in a car. Thank goodness, Violet was with you."

"It was a huge blessing." Molly carried the phone to the table and handed it to Nicole. "Well, it sounds like the Mortons didn't torch the barn."

Nicole got her smartphone out of her purse. "I'll put your number in my phone now."

"No one knows I have it except for Violet. She's going to charge it for me at her office. Well, probably Luke knows."

"You're right about Jane and Don Morton. We know now they didn't have anything to do with the fire. They were in Cleveland living with Mrs. Morton's sister. That's where they are now. When the foreclosure happened, they didn't care and wanted to leave this area. They offered their condolences to you."

"I'm glad it wasn't them. I hated to think that losing the property would cause them to resort to setting a fire." Molly wished with her whole heart that the person could be found. She wanted to move on with her life, but not knowing who killed Caleb kept her awake many nights. At least, the nightmares of the fire itself had lessened. "With what I've learned about Caleb's past, I wonder if the arsonist could be someone from Masonville."

After Nicole finished the bread, she used the napkin to wipe her mouth. "I'm sorry it took me a while to get back to you about Mr. and Mrs. Morton. There was a fire in Seaman and they asked me to investigate it for arson."

"I hope no one died or was injured."

"No one was in the building at the time. And it wasn't arson. There's another reason I'm just now getting back to you. Before the recent fire, Justin and I made another trip to Masonville. Perry took us to the farms where Caleb had gone to as his assistant. Everyone liked Caleb. We did find out that Caleb had an accident during the time he drove a car. He wasn't sited for it and the other driver was injured when she hit Caleb's car. She had gone through a red light and Caleb pulled onto the street in front of her."

Molly took a wet cloth and cleaned Isaac's face and hands. As she lifted him out of the high chair, she said in a defeated voice, "I can't believe I keep learning more and more things about my husband. He definitely lived a different life before he met me."

"The woman died six months ago, and it wasn't because of the accident." Nicole leaned down and pulled a box out of the bag. "Is it okay if I give it to Isaac now?"

"*Ya*. It's sweet you brought him a gift."

"After all the bread and whoopie pies I've eaten here, it's the least I can do."

"Are you kidding? You created my website for free." Talking about the bread made Molly think about the loaf she gave to Jonathan. "My grandpa wanted to tell Jonathan goodbye yesterday. I sent a loaf of my cinnamon bread with him to give Jonathan."

Nicole removed the cube and blocks from the box. After she carefully removed the plastic wrapping, she put a shape into the proper slot and said, "This square block goes here."

Isaac grabbed another block and kept turning it around in his hand.

"You have a smart little boy. Look how he's studying that triangle block."

"I'll put him on the floor to play. He's still in his pajamas because this morning was busy with my grandparents leaving." After Molly placed Isaac on the floor, Nicole put the cube and blocks next to him.

When Nicole returned to her chair, Molly thought how Nicole had called Dr. Knupp by his first name, and wondered if she was interested in him.

Nicole pretended to fan herself with her hand. "That Jonathan is one hot guy."

Molly rolled her eyes at Nicole. "That's something you mentioned Jonathan. I thought that you are interested in Dr. Knupp. You called him Perry. He's good-looking too."

"First, let's talk about Jonathan." Nicole gave her a serious look. "I know it's only been three months since Caleb died, but I can tell Jonathan is crazy about you. He wasn't here just to farm."

Molly shrugged. "We are friends, but it can't be anything more. I don't want to get married again." She didn't need to mention why a wedding wouldn't be in her future. Molly was disillusioned about men, one in particular, whenever she thought about marriage.

"I've known Jonathan ever since he moved here. Our paths have crossed with him being on the fire scenes as a firefighter. He's a wonderful man." Nicole glanced at Isaac. "He thinks the world of Isaac."

"My *daed* and grandfather both mentioned to me that Jonathan doesn't have a colorful past like Caleb. The bishop in Kenton knew the Mast family for years. Jonathan lived there until his parents moved to Wisconsin." Molly twisted her *kapp* tie around her finger, thinking about Jonathan. She did have feelings for him, but couldn't admit it to anyone. She shouldn't be thinking about him when Caleb hadn't been gone for long. Besides, she didn't need a husband and could make it on her own.

"There's something I want to ask you." Nicole picked a piece of lint off her navy blue blouse. "Perry asked me out for dinner. I didn't give him an answer. Would it bother you if I started seeing him?"

"You definitely should go out with him. It won't bother me. Besides, Anna works for him and she told me how he has taught her a lot. Of course, that doesn't sit well with my parents. They don't want her to go to college and become a veterinarian. But I think it's good because she will not be happy being a traditional Amish wife. She definitely wants to continue being an assistant."

"Could she delay baptism so she could go to college?"

"I suppose she could but if she goes away to college, I don't think she will want to become Amish. She'll have too much invested in the English world." Molly smiled, watching Isaac play. "He loves what you brought him."

"I'm glad. I should be going. After all, it is a work day." Nicole grinned at her. "I lose track of time when I'm with you and Isaac."

After Nicole stood, Molly picked up the empty cup. "You should go see Perry. He and Anna are at my parents' farm. One of the heifers was ready to deliver so Anna left. A previous calf died from this cow, so they want to have a healthy calf this time."

Nicole lifted Isaac and held him. "Maybe I will go see Perry. First, I have to get some hugging time in with my favorite baby."

Isaac grabbed a lock of Nicole's blonde hair. "Purty hair."

Nicole chuckled. "What a charmer. He's already giving compliments."

"I almost forgot to tell you the good news. Chloe Parrish's mom bought a quilt. She wants to give it to Chloe for a wedding gift. Chloe had planned to wait until she turned twenty to marry Dr. Tony, but she decided to have a summer wedding. I'm glad you gave that cube toy to Isaac. I need to get the quilt done. I might use the Pack 'n Play and put him in it to have fun with his new toy while I work on the quilt. Then in the afternoon, he takes a nap."

"When is the wedding?"

"July. I'm lucky that she liked a quilt I already have partially finished, but still I don't have much time."

Nicole raised her eyebrows. "Doesn't she live in Cincinnati? Were you able to send her a picture of the quilt?"

Molly nodded. "Violet took a picture of it with her phone and sent it to her in a text."

"You're getting phone savvy."

"Well, not really because I had Violet's help. And my little cell phone is for emergencies." She didn't want Nicole to get the impression that she didn't respect the *Ordnung's* rules for phones. Her faith was important to her, and she understood the reason for keeping a phone out of the home. Telephones represented a direct line to the world. Her *daed* liked to quote Romans 12:2 to his children to remind them they were to keep separate from the world: "Do not conform to the pattern of this world, but be transformed by the renewing of your mind. Then you will be able to test and approve what God's will is—his good, pleasing and perfect will."

Chapter Fourteen

Molly squeezed ketchup into her pan of browned hamburger. She decided to make sloppy joes for supper and have her mother's potato salad. When her mother dropped off Anna, she'd given a bowl of her potato salad. Apparently, she'd made a lot of it. Molly loved her *mamm's* potato salad. She was especially grateful to have the salad because Jonathan had called her last night. Because he didn't like to leave personal messages on her shared landline phone, he had called on her cell phone. Jonathan had wanted to know if he could stop by after work. He had something to give her, so she decided to invite him to supper.

Baked beans were in the oven for another dish. While she and Isaac were in Fields Corner in the morning, she'd bought a carrot cake from Weaver's Bakery. After working all day in construction, she was sure Jonathan would be starved.

Anna carried Isaac into the kitchen. "Molly, I'm going to Schumacher's house this evening to play volleyball. There are going to be a lot of kids there. It should be fun."

She sighed as she put the ketchup bottle on the kitchen counter. She turned away from the stove to give Anna her full attention. How could her little sister already be old enough to attend youth activities? Well, of course she was. Shortly after eighth grade graduation, she had started to work for Dr. Haney and now was Dr. Knupp's assistant. Anna was a few inches taller than she was. Like Luke and Beth, she had brown hair and brown eyes. Anna looked cute in a light green dress, and it was nice to see Anna wearing Amish clothing. She seemed to prefer jeans and a T-shirt, when she went on calls with Dr. Knupp. Their father had recently instructed Anna to only appear in jeans when she trained horses at their house. She wondered if that was one reason Anna had volunteered to stay with her. She might want to continue to wear the popular English jeans as often as possible. Molly had seen Anna's friends wear jeans sometimes, too, in their *rumspringa*.

"When did you grow up so fast? I remember you playing with dolls."

Anna rolled her brown eyes at her. "Geez, that was a long time ago, sis."

"Did you check with *Mamm* and *Daed* about going to Schumacher's house?" Although the Schumacher family attended a Mennonite church, they had invited Amish teens in the past to their house for youth activities. Before they married, Beth and Henry had gone there to play volleyball. Still she needed to make sure it was okay for Anna to go.

"You're getting heavy, Isaac. *Aenti's* going to put you down." After Anna put him on the floor, she handed him his sippy cup. She straightened her back. "I don't know how you carry him around plus you have another *boppli* in your belly."

"Are you trying to avoid answering my question? Did you get permission to go this evening?"

"I did. I ran outside after *Mamm* before she left here. She sure seemed in a rush to get to Beth's house. *Mamm* said it was fine as long as I didn't allow a Mennonite young man to take me home. I told her I'm going with Susan and her brother. They will bring me home too."

"That's *gut* you have a ride." Isaac dropped his cup and milk spilled onto the floor. Molly tore off a piece of paper towel and gave it to her son. "Please wipe up the milk."

Anna picked up the cup. "We don't want more milk on the floor. Whenever I'm here, I can cook for us. I do have some domestic skills. Just don't ask me to help work on your quilts. I don't like sewing."

Molly grinned. "*Ya*, I remember when I tried to interest you in sewing. You said it was boring, and horses were more interesting than looking at a piece of fabric."

Anna smoothed her black apron. "I know I'm different from all my sisters, but I like it this way. For a time, I even thought about asking Luke if I could work in his buggy shop. I'm not sure anymore about what to do with my life. I think I like training horses the most."

"I'm sure you'll figure it out. Pray and God will work it all out for you. He'll direct you with a feeling of peace when you make your decision."

"I hope so." Anna picked Isaac up. "Let's get you in your high chair. "We're going to eat soon."

Molly turned to stir the meat mixture and asked, "Has Dr. Knupp ever mentioned Caleb to you?"

"Not too much except that he was sorry that Caleb died. He asked once if you were doing okay financially. I told Perry that he could give me a raise if he wanted, so that I could help you with money."

Molly quickly turned to look at her sister. "Anna King, I hope you didn't say that to him."

Anna grinned. "*Ya*, I did. He laughed and said he was already paying me too much."

"I don't suppose you've met his sister, have you?"

"I haven't met her. I'm sure she's not as pretty as you are. Besides, Caleb married you. That's what is important."

At the sound of a buggy on the gravel, Molly ran to the window. When she saw it was Jonathan, she asked Anna, "Do I look okay?"

Anna arched her eyebrows. "I'm guessing it's Jonathan who is out there. You look pretty. Is that dress new?"

"*Ya*, Priscilla made it for me. I changed to it because my other dress felt tight. My baby's growing." She didn't need to tell her sister how she'd taken a quick shower before putting a clean dress on. Glancing down at her dress, she wanted to make sure it and apron were still clean. When she'd poured off the meat grease, she had been extra careful. Her clothing looked spotless and that was a miracle with Isaac usually getting her dirty. "*Ya*, it's Jonathan but we are only friends. I invited him to supper. He's worked hard here getting the crops planted. Could you put food on a plate for Isaac?"

"Sure. I'll do that."

As Anna put food on Isaac's blue plastic plate, Molly went to the door. She couldn't wait to see what he'd brought her and saw him standing next to his horse. *He looked good. Tall and broad shouldered and incredibly handsome. He wore a light blue shirt with his dark pants and suspenders.*

When he tethered Ginger, Jonathan noticed Molly and stared at her. In a loud voice, he said, "Sorry I forgot your gift."

"I forgot to cook supper," she quickly said.

"I better look and see if I did remember it." He leaned inside his buggy and once he was out again, she saw a fancy paper around something.

After Jonathan stood close to her, he handed her his gift.

She carefully removed the paper surrounding the vase. Molly was speechless as she held the heavy vase with an assortment of different colored roses and baby's breath.

"Do you like roses?"

"*Ya.* The roses are lovely. I like that you didn't choose one color but several. And the vase is wonderful too." She sniffed the flowers, and a look of pleasure crossed her face. "*Ach, danki.* I have never received flowers before."

"I gave the order yesterday and went today to get the flowers. I wanted them to be fresh."

* * *

At eight o'clock, it was just the two of them. Jonathan couldn't leave Molly. He knew it wasn't proper to stay when Anna had left, but he wanted to enjoy time alone with Molly. Maybe she felt the same way because she never mentioned that he should leave. In the living room, they sat on the sofa together and ate another piece of carrot cake. *Really, Anna just left an hour ago,* Jonathan thought. *No reason to feel concern that I'm still here.*

"You started to tell me about your house before I put Isaac to bed." Molly picked up her fork and jabbed a piece of cake. "I love the cream cheese frosting."

"It's *appeditlich*. Carrot cake is one of my favorite desserts."

She swallowed her bite of cake. "I'm glad I bought it then. My grandfather said that you have a full basement instead of a removable wall for church. What a clever idea."

He nodded. "It will make it easier when I have church in my home."

"My grandparents said when they were in Florida that they attended church services in a building instead of a home. Apparently, the Pinecraft Amish residences are too small to have church."

"I'd like to go there someday." He grinned. "Before I'm a senior citizen."

"Well, you have plenty of time before you're that old." She studied him for a moment. "I'm guessing you're twenty-five."

He chuckled. "Ray told you my age."

She finished her cake and lifted her cup of *kaffi* to her lips. "He did and was impressed you are able to build such a nice house debt-free."

"The labor part is free because I plan to help the other men with their home projects."

"I'm glad you have people to work with you on the house. It makes it nice so that you don't have to do it yourself."

"When I lived with my parents, I gave them money out of each paycheck. Here, my *daed* surprised me when he gave me all the money I'd given them through the years. I used this money to buy the lumber and other building materials. I didn't have any reason to stay in Kenton with my family moving. I thought about going with them, but Wisconsin winters sounded too cold to me. Then I saw this farm for sale at a good price."

She sent a perplexed look in his direction.

"What? You don't think I got a good deal?"

"It's not that. I'm amazed you didn't fall in love with someone from your hometown." She waved her fork at him. "Don't let this go to your head, but you are a reasonably attractive man. I imagine there were several women interested in you."

He smiled. "*Danki* for the compliment. When I was younger, I went to youth singings, but I stopped going a few years ago. I never found anyone I wanted to spend my life with."

"I'm glad you moved here. You're a *gut* neighbor." She gave him a shy glance. "I love the flowers and vase you gave me."

Although he was glad she loved his gift, Jonathan wished the spoken words were instead about her love for him. He'd be the happiest man in the world if she also could love him. Would she in time want to spend her life with him? He better snap out of it and say something. "I appreciated you sending my favorite bread with Ray."

She placed her empty plate on the end table "I can't get over how Caleb had a fiancée, and they were expecting a baby. It's hard to believe that he lived a completely different life before he met me."

"I'm sorry he wasn't upfront with you, and you had to learn this way."

"I want to meet Stacie. I know it sounds crazy, but I desperately want to learn more about the English Caleb. Obviously, he kept me in the dark about many things. I'm curious what he looked like when he lived away from our Plain community. I'm sure Stacie must have pictures of them as a couple. I want to see how happy he looked when he was with Stacie. Maybe he loved her more, but then he realized the path he had to take was the Amish one." Her expressive blue eyes filled with tears. "And I fit the bill."

"I'm sure that isn't how he felt. Caleb loved you. You are the most beautiful woman I know on the inside as well as the outside." Jonathan noticed the blush that bloomed on Molly's cheeks after he paid her the compliment.

She gave a nervous laugh. "I don't feel beautiful but *danki*."

He wanted his hands free so he put his plate on the table. He grasped her delicate hand in his. He noticed the warmness of her palm, and he didn't want to let go. "I'm glad I followed God's urging to move here. Meeting you has been the best thing to happen to me. I'm hoping you have feelings for me, and sometime, when the time's right for you, I'd like to date you."

"I feel guilty because I do have feelings for you," Molly said. "It's been such a short time since Caleb died."

Her voice held a breathless quality, and she suddenly gave him a startled glance.

"What is it?"

She gave him a small smile and moved his hand to touch a spot on her pregnant belly. "The baby is kicking hard. Usually, his movements are not this hard."

"I wonder if it's the baby's foot or hand moving so much." He raised his head and saw Molly's wistful expression. Maybe she regretted having him touch her belly. She might have decided it was too intimate when he wasn't her husband. "I'm sorry Caleb's not here to experience the baby's movements."

"I admit I was thinking how thrilled Caleb was when he felt Isaac's movements."

When he removed his hand from her pregnant belly, she slipped her hand into his. "I'm glad you were here to feel my active baby. After the baby's born, you might change your mind about dating me."

He squeezed her hand. "I'll never change my mind about you, Molly. I love you and I have never felt this way before. I already love Isaac."

Her eyes filled with humor. "I do have another option. Levi stopped in last week again to see if I needed anything. He's eager for a *fraa* and a mother for his children."

"Levi is a fine man and a deacon—"

"*Ach*, hush. I am never going to be serious about Levi." She pulled her hand away. "I'm glad you have been honest about how you feel, but I need to focus right now on my new quilt business. I want to be successful at it and to be able to make my house payments. I need to feel I can take care of my family before I even think about marriage. And I have some problem with thinking about marriage again after all the secrets Caleb kept from me. What I'm trying to say is I definitely need more time before I can commit to a relationship."

He nodded. "I'm *froh* to give you all the time you need."

"It's also hard to move on when I don't know who killed Caleb. Nicole has eliminated the former owners of this house as suspects in the fire." She twisted a prayer *kapp* tie around her finger. "I wonder now if a young man who tried to run Caleb and me off the road was angry enough to start a fire. He seemed to hate Amish people."

Jonathan couldn't believe what he just heard. Could it be the same man who was also angry at him for being Plain? "When I was outside the florist shop, a young man started yelling at me. He accused my horse of making a mess by his car, but it was a pile of potting soil. He had a white car and dark hair. He said that he wished we would live elsewhere."

"It could be the same man. I remember he drove a white car. Did you notice anything else?"

"A woman apologized for his behavior and said he was her brother. I didn't notice anything else."

"I'm going to call Nicole. It's not much to go on but maybe he's the arsonist."

"I should talk to her too."

CHAPTER FIFTEEN

As Perry drove to Nicole's apartment, he wondered if she would want to go out with him again. It seemed the evening had gone well. They went to a small Mexican restaurant that had opened a month ago in Fields Corner. While they ate enchiladas and rice, he'd enjoyed hearing about Nicole's former experience as a firefighter. She liked her career now as an arson investigator, but she was disappointed that the Ebersol case remained unsolved. She admitted that she and Detective Benning were no further ahead on the case, but there were no witnesses to the barn fire and no forensic evidence. She told Perry briefly about a recent fire at another barn, but there wasn't a connection to the Ebersol's fire. A group of teenagers smoking pot had started it. They had tried to put the fire out themselves before anyone had called the fire department.

He glanced at Nicole and thought how lovely she was with her green eyes and her blonde hair tumbling around her shoulders. She wore a white and aqua striped dress. He was glad that he'd made the trip back home to take a shower. Taking her out in his smelly clothes after helping a cow deliver a calf would not have made a good impression for a first date. He was glad that he decided to wear dress pants and a new shirt he'd gotten from Mia for his birthday.

When her cell phone rang, she removed it from her bag and glanced at the screen. "I wonder why Jonathan is calling me. I hope nothing is wrong with Molly. I better answer it."

From Nicole's end of the conversation, Perry realized that it wasn't Jonathan calling.

"Molly, that's good you're using Jonathan's cell phone. You should save your minutes. You might need the minutes for Isaac or when you go into labor. I agree with you." Nicole was quiet for a moment and then said, "I'm glad you told him about the white car and that awful man who had road rage against you. It sounds like he could be guilty. Okay, I'll get more information from Jonathan."

When Nicole said "guilty", Perry thought how Molly must have information that could help with the case. After he pulled his car into the spot next to Nicole's car, he pushed the button to turn off the engine.

He saw her pull a small pad and pen out of her purse. Before jotting anything down, she switched the phone to her left ear. After she wrote for a few seconds, Nicole said, "Jonathan, this might be the lead we need. I'll go in the morning to see the owner at the florist shop. I hope that the sister paid for the flowers with a credit card. Thanks for the descriptions of both the brother and sister. You said the man's name was Jeff, right?" She scrawled the name on her writing pad.

When she chuckled, Perry wondered what Jonathan said that was funny. *I hope Nicole fills me in about the new lead she has.*

After Nicole said goodbye, she dropped her phone on her lap. While she wrote a few more things on her pad, Nicole said, "Molly told me that there had been an incident when Caleb was still alive, and they were going home one evening in their buggy. A man drove his car beside them and yelled swear words to them. He definitely didn't have any love for them. He said their horses and buggies shouldn't be on the roads."

"Does Jonathan think he knows this man?"

Nicole nodded, turning her head to look at him. "This might be the breakthrough I've been praying for. Jonathan went to the florist to pick out flowers and a vase for Molly. This man called Jeff complained to Jonathan about his horse taking a dump by his car."

"Is that why you laughed?"

"I laughed because Jonathan said it was potting soil, but Jeff didn't believe him. He criticized Amish people and how he wished they didn't live here. After Jeff's sister came out of the florist shop with a bouquet, she apologized to Jonathan for her brother. When Molly mentioned to Jonathan about the white car and the man, he realized Jeff could have been angry enough to start the fire. He drives a white car." Nicole touched his arm. "Would you like to come in for coffee? I have decaffeinated. I'll make a quick call to Justin and tell him what I learned."

"Coffee sounds good. While you call Justin, I can look up to see what time the shop opens in the morning." He definitely wanted to go in her apartment and spend more time with Nicole. She was easy to talk to and was a good listener. He quickly got out of the car and opened her door.

"Thank you, Perry." After she dropped her pad and phone in her purse, she got out of the car.

While Nicole used her Keurig to fix their cups of coffee, he sat on the sofa facing her small kitchen. After he found Donna's Florist Shop on his smartphone, he said, "The shop opens at eight o'clock tomorrow."

"That's great. I'm going to go ahead and call Justin. How do you take your coffee?"

"Black."

After a few minutes, she finished her phone conversation with the detective and joined Perry on the sofa. She sipped her coffee. "Whew, what an evening this turned out to be. I'm hoping we can give Molly closure soon. Knowing who did this crime won't bring Caleb back, but at least she will know who did this terrible act."

"If this Jeff did start the fire, it appears he did it because he dislikes the Amish. But why did he choose to torch Caleb's barn instead of another farmer's barn?"

Nicole ran her finger around the cup rim. "That's what Justin and I wonder. Caleb had a car accident, but he wasn't sited for it. The other driver was injured. That could be a connection that caused Jeff to want revenge. Of course, this is all speculation. We might not be on the right track, but then again maybe Jeff is the arsonist."

He grinned. "It's a good thing Jonathan bought flowers when he did. Now you have a chance to solve the case."

Nicole frowned. "I just don't get why some people have it in for the Plain people. They are peaceful and loving."

"I agree. I've enjoyed meeting more of the Amish farmers with taking Dr. Haney's place. I wish, though, Caleb had been honest about his background. I still would've hired him."

"He seemed intent on keeping his Amish life a secret from you and Stacie. And poor Molly. I hated each time I had to tell her something about Caleb's past that she didn't already know. I hope she can learn to trust a man again." Nicole put her cup on the coffee table. "I forgot. I have whoopie pies. Would you like one? They are delicious. Molly gave them to me."

"That sounds good. I'm hooked on Amish food and their desserts. I want to take Stacie and Mia sometime to go to the stores in Fields Corner."

Nicole put her blonde hair behind her ears. "Molly wants to meet you and Stacie sometime. She wonders if there is anything else about Caleb that she doesn't know."

He shrugged. "I don't think there is anything else to tell her. From what Anna has mentioned, it sounds like Molly knows everything about Caleb during the time he worked for me. I can stop sometime when I drop Anna off at Molly's. She's staying at Molly's house now since their grandparents left."

Nicole put the chocolate whoopie pies on a plate and returned to the sofa. "I'm sorry that Caleb died, but something good came out of it. Meeting Molly has enriched my life. We've become good friends. And I love her little boy, Isaac."

"I'm glad we didn't eat dessert at the restaurant. These whoopie pies are huge." He picked up one of the chocolate pies. "I'm sure she feels the same way about you. It's great you did a website for her. Anna said that gave Molly something positive to focus on."

"Well, I enjoyed creating the website. I don't feel like I have done as much for her as someone else has. I haven't given money to Molly. Did you hear how an anonymous person gave a thousand dollars to Molly?"

Weird that Nicole is mentioning the money I gave. Is she messing with me and knows it's me? But how could she? "I'm sure Molly can use the money." After Perry swallowed a bite of his pie, he said, "I took home a dozen whoopie pies last week. Mia and Stacie loved them."

Nicole ignored his food comment and said, "The same person gave money to the Weavers for the food for the barn raising. I'm not talking about a little money, but enough to pay for the food for the whole week for the barn workers. Also money was given for the lumber for the new barn."

"That was thoughtful for someone to do that for Molly. Maybe it wasn't the same person."

"I saw all three notes. The handwriting was identical." Nicole's eyes narrowed as she stared at him. "I'm thinking the person must have been close to Caleb at one time."

"Or maybe close to Molly and felt sorry she was a widow with a young baby." *Does Nicole think I gave the money? It sure seems like she's hinting that I'm the donor.*

When Nicole laughed, he sighed. *I don't have to tell her that I gave the money because I suspected Stacie of starting the fire. I never want my sister to know that I ever thought she could do something so horrible.* "You got me. How did you figure it out I was the one who gave the money? Did you recognize my handwriting?"

"Hey, I'm an investigator, remember?" Nicole grinned. "Truthfully, it just hit me today that you're such a kind person and you cared for Caleb. Sure, you hated how he treated Stacie, but he still had been your friend and employee. I considered how you gave your time to help with the barn raising. Then this evening I peeked at your signature when you signed the credit card slip for our dinner."

Leaning closer to her on the sofa, he smiled at her. "Since you're such a clever woman, what do you think I'm going to do next?"

She gave him a playful wink and said softly, "I know what I'd like for you to do, but I'm not sure that's what you have in mind."

He hadn't planned to kiss her already on their first date, but it was obvious that she wanted to kiss him. She must feel the attraction between them too. He tossed his uneaten whoopie pie on the plate and pulled her into his arms. Perry's heart raced wildly. Holding her ignited all kinds of wonderful feelings inside him. He lowered his head slightly and touched his lips to hers. When she kissed him back, energy surged through him.

He wasn't surprised that Nicole tasted as great as she smelled. She wore a sweet perfume and her mouth was soft and warm from the coffee she had sipped. Her lip gloss tasted of peppermint. Everything about Nicole was perfect. It'd been five long years since he'd felt this way about a woman.

After they stopped kissing, Nicole asked, "How much longer do you think you will have to cover for Dr. Haney?"

At first, he was stunned by her question. He hadn't expected her to ask how soon he'd be done in Fields Corner. Maybe she liked him being in her town occasionally. "It was originally only supposed to be for a couple of weeks because another veterinarian was going to fill in for Dr. Haney. He hasn't been able to do it. I did hear that Dr. Haney's surgery went well. He should be back in another month."

"I'm glad Dr. Haney is healing okay."

Nicole sounded disappointed. *She must want to see me again*, he thought. "It's been good for me to take over Dr. Haney's practice. I've enjoyed getting to know the Amish farmers who have needed my services for their animals, but more importantly I've liked seeing you."

"When Justin and I went to Masonville, it took us around forty-five minutes from Fields Corner."

He nodded. "It's not too far for me to drive to see you. I'd like to go out again."

"I can drive sometimes to Masonville. I'd like to meet your daughter." She grinned. "I don't want to scare you off, but I'm twenty-nine years old. I'm hoping someday to have a husband and children."

"You aren't scaring me off. I was happily married, and had a wonderful life with Kathleen. I've never found anyone I wanted to get serious about until you."

CHAPTER SIXTEEN

After the phone call ended to Nicole, Jonathan related to Molly what the investigator had said.

"It's amazing you might have talked to the man who killed Caleb." Molly tucked a loose hair under her *kapp*. "Maybe soon I'll find out if it was hatred against the way we live, or if there was more to it. After learning about Caleb's secrets, I keep wondering if he caused someone to want revenge against him personally. It could be a past grudge."

"Maybe it involved both reasons." Jonathan leaned toward the table and grabbed his cup and plate. "I better leave. Tomorrow morning will come soon. *Danki* for the delicious supper and dessert."

"I should have fixed more. You work hard on your day job and on building your own house."

"It was plenty."

As they walked to the kitchen, Molly hated for the evening to end. It had been nice to spend time with Jonathan without anyone else in the house. Maybe too much. After all, she was a widow in the mourning period.

Once his hands were free of the dishes, Jonathan stared at her for a moment. Then he stepped closer to her and took her hands in his. She wanted him to put his arms around her, but realized that it wasn't proper for her to think like that. They were friends and nothing more. Taking a deep breath, she smelled his clean, masculine scent and liked how he towered over her.

"You look *schee* but then you always do."

Her face felt warm. Whenever she became embarrassed, she blushed. How could he think she looked pretty when she was as big as a house? Just that day when she had been in Weaver's Bakery buying the carrot cake, she heard an English woman say to another woman, "That Amish woman is huge. I wonder if she is pregnant with twins." She had been right behind the woman in line and thought how rude of her to mention how big she looked to her friend. Couldn't she have waited until she left the store and said it in private? She felt like tapping her on the shoulder and telling the Englisher that her pregnancy hadn't affected her hearing.

"*Danki*. You look nice," she said softly.

"After your mourning period ends, I'd like to date you. You don't need to give me an answer now and can think about it for later. I know I should wait until after your baby is born, because you have a lot on your mind now. While building my house, I think about how much I want you to be my *fraa*. I also want to be Isaac's father and the new baby's too."

Her body reacted strongly to him holding her hands. She was definitely attracted to him but maybe not as much as he appeared to be attracted to her. She saw the tenderness of his gaze. Although his words rang with deep emotion, was it right for her to tell him how she wanted to date him too? She had avoided thinking about being with Jonathan in a relationship until now. She had reminded herself many times that they were friends and nothing more. She stared at his dark hair and his hazel eyes. Not only was Jonathan handsome, but he was big and strong.

Her husband had been a big man too. *That's right, I should be remembering Caleb instead of thinking how good-looking Jonathan is,* she thought. *After all, Caleb has only been dead for a little over three months. Even though he hadn't been truthful about his past, I still love him.*

Jonathan dropped her hands. "I'm sorry. I shouldn't have said anything. It was wrong of me."

She shook her head so hard that her *kapp* ties bounced up and down on her shoulders. "I'm glad you did. I have strong feelings for you, but I admit I feel guilty that I do. Caleb hasn't been gone long. Right after I learned about Stacie and the other things, I told my *daed* that I couldn't trust another man enough to marry again. You have changed my mind somewhat, but I definitely need more time. And I need to focus on getting a lot done before the baby is born."

"I can wait on you. It doesn't matter how long you need. No pressure. If you should need any help with anything, let me know."

"You already have a full-time job, volunteer for the fire department, and are building a house. I don't want to give you more work."

"I always have time for you." He reached out and touched her cheek, running his finger along her cheekbone. "You have beautiful skin and it is so soft. I think I better go before I do something that I shouldn't."

He wants to kiss me, she thought.

After he grabbed his straw hat off the peg by the door, Jonathan said, "*Gut nacht*, Molly."

She smiled. "*Gut nacht.*"

Leaning against the closed door, she wondered if her pregnancy hormones were messing with her mind. Right at this moment, she desired to have a man in her life again. Was it because she didn't want to raise two *kinner* by herself? Or was the real reason because she was falling for Jonathan? But she should not be. It was way too soon.

Too much excitement for me to go to bed now, Molly thought. *I'll work on Chloe's quilt that Pam bought for her daughter. It was nice of her to pay the total amount for the quilt instead of giving me a deposit.*

She decided to check on Isaac, and was thankful she had baby monitors. They didn't use electricity and were battery powered. She picked up the monitor from the counter and saw how adorable Isaac looked sleeping. Her eyes filled and she blinked back tears. She was blessed to have such a *wunderbaar* child. *I can't wait to see how he reacts to the new baby. In some ways, it'd be nice for him to have a little brother but being a big brother to a sister would be nice for Isaac too.*

The active kicking from earlier must have worn the little one out. How could I have been so bold and put Jonathan's hand on my belly? That is something intimate for a husband to feel. I wasn't thinking and acted on an impulse. Is that why he decided to mention me be-

coming his wife in the future? No, he was obviously interested in me before this evening. I still can't believe he brought me flowers. What a thoughtful man!

After she placed the monitor back on the kitchen counter, Molly prayed, *Dear Lord, Thank You for bringing Jonathan into my life. He's been a great support to me while grieving. I already have strong feelings for Jonathan. If You want him to become more than a friend and eventually for me to be his wife, I need help in order to heal from losing Caleb. I want to do Your will in my life always. In Jesus' Name, I pray. Amen.*

* * *

Three days later, Nicole and Sheriff Lynch came to Molly's house. The sheriff was of medium height and looked to be in his forties. She remembered hearing he had a wife and four children. He was well-liked in their community because of his dedication and hard work.

After they were seated in the living room, Sheriff Lynch said, "I've arrested Jeff Ankrum for arson and for the murder of your husband. We found his gas-soaked clothes in his garage. It's hard to believe that he never got rid of the evidence. I wanted to let you know in person."

Molly knew they were both coming because Nicole had checked to see if she would be home in the morning. She appreciated them coming to her house instead of asking her to make the trip into town. Nicole had informed her the other day that she'd learned Jeff's last name and that they would be following up on him. He was definitely a person of interest she'd said.

After months wondering who the arsonist was, now she finally knew his name. She had to know why he did it. Leaning forward, she asked, "Why did he start the fire in our barn? Was it because we are Amish?"

Sheriff Lynch's eyes looked troubled. "I need to apologize to you. Soon after the fire, I thought of Jeff. When I questioned him, Jeff had an alibi that checked out. His sister said he was with her that night but he wasn't."

"She never thought he did it, so she lied for him." Nicole continued, "He told her that he was home sleeping."

Sheriff Lynch nodded. "I wish she hadn't lied. She interfered with our investigation. Caleb came to me after the incident with your buggy. Apparently, Jeff had done this a couple of other times to Caleb when he was in his buggy. When you and Isaac were in the buggy that particular night, Caleb decided that Ankrum was dangerous. He knew an Amish baby had died when teenagers threw bricks at their buggy. Even though the crime happened in another state, he was afraid that Ankrum might throw something at you sometime. Caleb decided to report him."

"I don't understand. How did Caleb know his name?"

"Caleb was driving his car when Mrs. Ankrum ran a red traffic light and hit him. When Jeff and the police came on the accident scene, she blamed Caleb for the accident. There were several witnesses that saw it happen, and they all claimed it was her fault. She also had been drinking." Sheriff Lynch ran his fingers through his sandy blond hair. "There's more. His father had owned a restaurant years ago in Fields Corner, but he wasn't a good business owner. He sold it to the Weavers. Later Mr. Ankrum committed suicide."

"Jeff's sister said that their mother had died several months ago from liver cancer," Nicole said. "Jeff was especially close to their mother. In his mind, a lot of their family troubles were a result of the Amish, and he blamed Caleb for his mother becoming more depressed after the accident. I know it doesn't make any sense that he felt this way. He was and is a very disturbed young man. He needed help for his mental illness. His sister said she should've made him go to a psychiatrist, but she never thought he'd be this cruel to commit arson."

Molly couldn't feel sympathy for Jeff Ankrum. He'd destroyed the life and love she and Caleb had shared together. Caleb hadn't deserved to die in a fire set by a crazy person. And why did people think using this for a reason should make it all right? "He must be mentally ill to have done all the things he has, but that doesn't make me feel better. Did he show any remorse for killing Caleb?"

Sheriff Lynch nodded his head. "Yes, he did. He never thought Caleb would get killed and was sorry he did. That doesn't change anything for Ankrum. He'll be tried for murder along with arson."

* * *

Outside in the warm sunshine, Molly and Nicole sat on a bench as they watched Anna pushing Isaac in his new swing. Isaac's chubby face was full of smiles.

"I'm glad you suggested coming outside." Molly liked that Nicole had driven separately and could stay after the sheriff had left. "I'm trying to wrap my head around the fact that someone could hate us this much. Of course, I've heard of other cases where Amish people have been victims of violence, but it's never happened here. Well, it did once when a young man tried to shoot Luke because he wanted to be with Violet. My brave sister-in-law jumped in front of Luke and took the bullet."

"It was scary when he held Violet hostage and shot her. I'm glad no one was killed."

"I remember how many of us drove our buggies to town. We lined up outside Angela's Restaurant and prayed for Violet and the other people inside."

"And now Violet is Amish. It all worked out." Nicole patted her arm. "I'm sorry that the fire happened. Things like this shouldn't happen to good people like you and your family. The Amish are peaceful and it is so sad. Ankrum will go to jail for a long time."

She hoped Nicole was right. It would be hard to see him in town if he shouldn't get a long prison sentence. "*Danki* for all your work on this case."

"You're welcome."

Molly had been thinking about telling Nicole she'd like her to be present for her baby's birth. Their friendship had been the one good thing to come out of the tragedy. It seemed like now would be a good time to mention it to her English friend. It was something positive to talk about and to make happy plans about the new baby. "I'm still planning on having a home birth. Since Violet's going to be my midwife, I won't even need a doctor present. She's a certified nurse-midwife now."

"Did you want me to take care of Isaac while you're in labor? I'll be happy to help." Nicole waved to Isaac. "He loves his swing."

"Jonathan bought it for him and put it on the tree." Molly grinned at her. "I never thought of asking you to do *that*, but I should have since you love Isaac so much. I'd like you to be here when I have the baby. You can think about it and don't have to let me know ahead of time. And I know you might not be able to make it anyhow with your job."

Nicole hugged her. "I'm thrilled you asked me. Yes, I'd love to be here when you have your baby. I'm honored that you want to include me."

Molly laughed. "I didn't expect you to be this excited."

"Hey, what about me?" Anna asked. "If Isaac is asleep, I can help Violet."

Molly looked at Anna. "That sounds perfect. *Mamm* and Priscilla will probably be here too, so one of them can watch Isaac. I'll tell Violet you might want to help."

As Anna took Isaac out of the swing, she said, "Maybe I should consider becoming a midwife instead of a veterinarian. Delivering human babies instead of animal babies could be more interesting."

Molly rolled her eyes at Anna. "I hope so."

"Do you know if you're having a boy or a girl?" Nicole asked.

Molly shook her head, remembering how Violet had mentioned doing an ultrasound in March. She'd told her that she'd rather wait. "I haven't had an ultrasound, but Violet wants me to next visit. But I don't want to know if it's a boy or a girl. I want to be surprised."

Anna carried Isaac to the bench and handed him to Nicole. "I've seen the jealousy in your green eyes while I pushed him. He's all yours. I'm going to check on Cinnamon."

Nicole kissed Isaac's forehead. "Geez, Anna, I didn't realize I was that obvious."

"Anna King, I know why you gave Isaac to Nicole. I smell something coming from his diaper."

"Let's go in the house." Molly stood. "I'll change his diaper while you tell me about your date with Perry."

Nicole gave her a broad smile. "I'll tell you about it on one condition."

"What's the condition?"

"That you tell me what occurred here after you received flowers from Jonathan."

CHAPTER SEVENTEEN

The next couple of months passed in a burst of activity. Molly kept busy playing with Isaac, visiting family, and finishing quilt orders. Luke mailed the quilts for her and used his post office box number. By July, she decided that she had enough money to take a break from her business. After all, she was due in two weeks. Nicole put the announcement on the website that no new orders would be taken until September. The crops looked good and there should be a plentiful harvest. She planned to give some of the money from the sale of the crops to Jonathan. He'd helped a lot with her farm.

The baby clothes were all washed and put in the chest of drawers. Jonathan moved the cradle that Isaac had slept in during the early months back into her bedroom. Her parents had given her the cradle that had been used for each of the King *kinner*. Beth hadn't wanted it because Henry had made a cradle for their first-born, Nora Marie, and they had a second antique cradle. When their twins, James and Julia, were born, they put them together in a crib instead of using the smaller cradles. Beth wanted the closeness they'd shared in the womb to continue during their first few months of infancy. Molly thought it was cute to see the twins sleeping in the same bed—James at one end of the crib and Julia at the other end.

On a hot, Saturday afternoon, Molly relaxed on the sofa and thought how the baby could come anytime because everything was ready for delivery. Violet had given her a list of supplies to have for the home birth. Every necessary item had been purchased. She had plenty of newborn diapers because of Caleb's *mamm*. The other day, Rose and Andy had visited her and Isaac. Rose gave her a diaper bag filled with disposable diapers, wipes, and a few small baby toys. For Isaac, they brought a red barn set with farm animals. It had been Caleb's favorite wooden toy when he'd been Isaac's age. When Andy got on the floor to play with his grandson, Molly felt moisture in her eyes.

Her thoughts were interrupted when she heard a car in the driveway. Glancing at the clock, she saw it was two o'clock, and Molly knew it probably would be Nicole. After her weekly doctor's appointment, Nicole had talked about stopping in on Saturday afternoon, and she'd called her a couple of hours ago to say she'd see her soon. It was only seconds after she'd heard the car that Nicole appeared on the front porch. Whenever Isaac took his afternoon nap, Molly rested in the living room. Nicole knew she liked sitting on the sofa with her legs propped up on a gray footstool. It matched Jonathan's new sofa but he'd given the ottoman to her to use.

On the other side of the door, stood her friend. "Hi, Nicole. Come on in."

Opening the screen door, she entered the room. "Oh my gosh, you look miserable."

"Geez, thanks. But you're right. I hate this hot, humid weather. Don't ever have a baby in July. Isaac was born in August and it was a very hot summer then too. There isn't even a breeze going through here today. If I open the front door and have the kitchen door open, there is sometimes a nice breeze that helps cool me off."

"I brought your popsicles as you requested." Nicole stood in front of her, and opened the box. "Which flavor do you want to start with?"

Molly laughed. "You know that I'll eat more than one this afternoon. I'll start with orange."

After she handed her an orange single popsicle, Nicole said, "I'll put the box in your freezer. When you want another one, I'll be your gopher."

"*Danki.* You're the best friend ever." *A cold popsicle might help to cool me off,* Molly thought. When Nicole had called earlier, she had asked if she could bring her anything. Molly told her if it wasn't too much trouble that she'd like popsicles.

"I'm glad you have a refrigerator with a top freezer compartment." Nicole called from the kitchen. "Good, there is room for the popsicles."

"I'm happy there is room for the box. I won't have to walk outside to my chest freezer." Caleb and she had gone together with a few families to keep electric freezers in a small building on an English neighbor's property. "That reminds me I need to pay the rental fee."

"That's nice you also have a bigger freezer."

"There is a pitcher of lemonade in the refrigerator. Pour yourself a glass."

"Lemonade sounds good. I'll bring you a glass of lemonade too."

Nicole put Molly's glass on the end table and sat next to her. "Are you sure you don't want to stay with me in my air-conditioned apartment? We also have a pool in the complex. We could go swimming. There's even a little kiddie pool that Isaac would love."

"It is tempting to stay with you, but I can't sleep at night anyhow. It's not just the heat. I can't get comfortable and I was miserable the last month with Isaac too. I remember how Caleb used to rub my back to help me sleep. If the barn hadn't been engulfed by flames and killed Caleb, he'd still be here to rub my back when I can't sleep." Her jaw dropped open. "I didn't mean that the way it sounded. I don't want him to be here just so he could rub my back. I miss him and it makes me feel bad that Isaac will be too young to remember him and the baby won't ever know his or her father."

"I knew what you meant. That was sweet of Caleb to rub your back. I'm sorry he's not here."

"If Caleb had never lived in Masonville, he might still be alive. He could've worked with Dr. Haney and lived with his parents. Then the accident with Ankrum's mother never would've happened. Maybe then Ankrum wouldn't have chosen our barn to burn." She needed to stop talking what could have been. Clearing her throat, she continued, "But I'm thankful for the time we had together."

"You're such a strong and amazing woman to keep going in spite of everything."

"My faith gives me strength. And God has blessed me with a *wunderbaar gut* family and friends like you."

"And Jonathan. Isn't he your friend?"

Molly rolled her eyes at Nicole. "*Ya*, you know he is a *gut* friend."

"You're thirty-seven weeks now so it should be any day."

"I hope so. I'm ready to greet my new baby. Violet wants me and Isaac to stay with her and Luke. They've moved into their house so there's plenty of room. Hannah decided to rent their apartment." Molly took a bite of her popsicle, thinking she better eat it faster. It might drip on her. "Violet's afraid I'll have a short labor with it being my second one. Isaac came quickly but I did have back labor all night with him. I was too stupid to realize when my back hurt so much that I was in labor."

"Maybe you should stay at Violet's. It definitely would be convenient being close to your midwife."

Molly shrugged. "I'd rather still stay here. Besides, Violet and Luke are still newlyweds."

Nicole sipped her lemonade. "I'll buy you some battery-run fans."

"Did I tell you about Jonathan's house? He's been taking me and Anna to see the progress on it. It should be completely finished soon. Simon Yoder is making the kitchen cabinets. It's a beautiful house. I love how the basement is built into the bank of the hill. The soil around the basement is cooler than the air temperature and insulates the basement; it will keep it cooler in the summer and warmer in the winter. Jonathan's going to put a kitchen in the basement too. That way in the summer canning and cooking can be done in the basement."

Nicole grinned. "That's terrific you like it. I think Jonathan has been giving you tours and asking for your advice for a good reason . . . he's hoping you'll be living in the house someday. He wants you to love it."

She smiled back at Nicole. "You might be onto something. I didn't tell you or anyone, but a couple of months ago, Jonathan mentioned that he wants to marry me."

Nicole's eyebrows shot up and in an indignant voice, she said, "And you've kept this from me. I bet Jonathan asked you when he gave you the flowers. I knew you weren't telling me everything. I'll forgive you since you're telling me now. Did you give him the answer he wanted?"

She hadn't told anyone because it hadn't seemed right to talk about marrying Jonathan. How could she say yes when she was carrying Caleb's baby? And she had been a widow for such a short time. "I couldn't say yes. I told Jonathan I needed more time. He said he would wait and there wasn't any pressure for me to give him an answer yet."

"I understand and that makes sense."

"I seem to have a lot of visitors these days. Even Levi Lantz came yesterday."

Nicole chuckled. "He is a persistent man. I'd think he'd realize by now how much you care for Jonathan."

In the past, Molly had shared with Nicole that Levi seemed interested in her becoming his wife. "Levi asked if there was even a small chance I might want to marry him in the near future. I told him that we would never be a couple. In some ways, it would be for the best if I married Levi."

Nicole gave her a puzzled look. "Why do you think that? You've complained that Levi is a pest when he comes to see you."

She might as well mention a fear she had if Jonathan became her husband. "I'm afraid of what might happen if I marry Jonathan. He could die in a fire. I can't go through that pain again of losing someone I love so much. I don't love Levi, but maybe in time I could love him. He doesn't run the risk of dying whenever there is a fire. He's never going to be a firefighter. Jonathan's volunteer job scares me that he'll rush into a burning building and he will lose his life."

Nicole let out an exasperating sigh. "That could happen but Jonathan is an excellent firefighter. I don't think that should be a reason not to marry him. And I think he would quit volunteering if you told him how you feel about it. By the way, there seems to be more deaths from buggy accidents in this area, then from fire deaths. Levi could easily die in a buggy accident."

"Unfortunately, it does happen too often. Some Amish residents are not allowed to use blinkers; they instead often use kerosene lights, which are hard to see. I have a blinker and two LED lights on my buggy so that makes me safer. More accidents in these communities occur when they relay on the kerosene lights. Levi told me about a widow he met recently. Her husband and two *kinner* died in a buggy accident. She and one son survived. He's considering dating her. I told him he should."

"It sounds like she is his second choice. I hope it works out for both of them."

Molly picked up a hand fan and started moving it rapidly in front of her face. After a minute of fanning herself, she said, "This isn't helping much. I asked Violet why the heat has to be so hard on pregnant women when in the last stretch of pregnancy. Violet said that my body has to do more work with the baby being larger now. She said that my body is also managing my baby's nutrients. This extra work causes me to feel overheated. It is definitely something bringing a new life into the world. I understand the labor pain part of childbirth because of Eve and what she did in the Garden of Eden. But Jesus in his wonderful wisdom taught in the book of John that once the woman has given birth to her child, she will no longer remember the anguish because she will have joy that a human being has been born into the world. And it's true because I did forget the actual labor pain with Isaac."

"Well, you're amazing. I hope you have an easy time of it. I can't wait to see the baby. I can't believe how you haven't gained anywhere except where the baby is. My sister's face got fuller and she gained weight all over when she was pregnant." Nicole pulled two small wrapped packages from a Target bag. "I have a small gift for the baby from Stacie. She also bought a book for Isaac. She remembered you said that his birthday is in August."

As she tore off the paper, Molly was glad that in June she'd met Caleb's former fiancée. At her request, Stacie had visited her and Isaac when Perry came to Fields Corner to go to a nearby farm. He'd dropped off his sister and picked up Anna to go with him. Meeting Stacie helped Molly to move on about that chapter in

Caleb's life. Stacie had brought a few photographs of them as a couple. The English Caleb in the pictures surprised her with his short haircut and his non-Amish clothing. She liked the looks of her Caleb better. He was meant to join the Amish church and to marry her.

The box contained an assortment of colorful bibs and baby socks. "The bibs are adorable. Tell her thank you for me. I'm glad I met Stacie, especially since it looks like you and Perry are dating. It's my turn to ask for an update about you two."

Nicole grinned. "Perry is crazy about me and I feel the same way about him. There might be a wedding next year."

"I'm happy to hear that. Perry's a great guy."

Nicole laughed. "I'm not surprised you feel that way. I never should have admitted he was the one who gave money to you. I think that has colored your impression of him, but you're absolutely right. Perry's a marvelous man and I already love him."

Molly enjoyed seeing her friend happy. "Well, you couldn't lie to a bishop's daughter. Hey, when Anna showed me his handwriting, I knew it had to be Perry."

"He said when he wrote the notes, he wasn't expecting to be working here in Fields Corner and for us to have a chance to see his handwriting."

Molly put the gift box on the sofa next to the bag and slowly stood. "I'm going to get another popsicle. Can I get you something? I baked chocolate chip cookies this morning before it got hot."

"I better not. I haven't had time to run as much this week."

"You don't need to lose any weight." Molly looked closely at Nicole and thought how thin she looked in her tan capris and a white and green top.

"Perry and I are invited to have dinner with friends of his this evening. I better save room for it."

CHAPTER EIGHTEEN

After work on Monday, Jonathan pulled into Molly's driveway. He had picked wildflowers for her because he thought she might like the orange lilies and white daisies. They reminded him of Molly because she was vibrant, strong, yet fragile. . . like the flowers. Although she didn't wear perfume like some English women, she always smelled sweet and womanly like a field of fragrant flowers. He'd been taking her little gifts, and didn't care if it wasn't proper. He could court the woman he loved in private. When the time was right, he hoped Molly would agree to marry him.

As he tied Ginger to the post, he thought how the battery-run fans had pleased Molly. When he'd seen Nicole in the Walmart store, she'd mentioned looking for battery-run fans. He'd offered to take the fans to Molly. Nicole had a date with Perry so she accepted his help. Molly's eyes had widened with surprise when he'd taken the two fans to her on Saturday. She couldn't believe that Nicole had gone to the store straight from her house. Molly said that he was wonderful to bring them to her so quickly.

As he went back to the buggy to retrieve the bouquet, he prayed softly, "Lord, I give thanks to You for nudging me to move to Fields Corner. Meeting Molly has been a *wunderbaar* blessing to me. I will try to listen and to continue to follow Your direction for my life. Help me to be patient about Molly. I'm anxious for her to be my *fraa*. In Your Name, I pray. Amen."

Suddenly Molly stood on the back porch, holding a squirming Isaac. "Jonathan, I'm glad you're here. I'm in labor. Could you watch Isaac until the women arrive?"

Once on the porch, he grabbed Isaac. "Let's go put the flowers in water for your *mamm*."

"Okay, Jon-Jon," Isaac smiled, grinning.

He loved how Isaac had created a name for him that he could say. "How close are your contractions?"

"They are already pretty close together. I called Violet, my *mamm*, and Nicole as soon as I felt the first one. I wanted to give everyone time to get here, but now I'm worried they might not make it."

He followed Molly into the kitchen and put Isaac on the floor. Before he could ask if he could do anything else for her, he saw how swiftly Molly's face became grim. She gripped the end of the table as her mouth tightened.

What should I do? Take Isaac to another room? Or stay here with Molly?

* * *

Violet grinned at Molly. "How was it having your baby in an actual bed instead of on the back seat of my car? I know it was much better for me."

Propped up with pillows against the bed headboard, Molly glanced from Violet to her infant girl. Her daughter lay nestled firmly in the crook of her arm. Looking down at her baby's little head covered with dark hair, she thought how her face was perfect. Isaac's features had been a little smashed looking from being the first baby to enter her birth canal. "Your *Aenti* Violet thinks she is funny, but it's okay because she's a terrific midwife."

Her *mamm* nodded. "*Ya*, Violet is the best. I wish Anna had been here instead of off with Dr. Haney."

"Anna's serious about becoming a midwife, and she plans to quit soon working with Dr. Haney," Violet said, as she moved about the other side of the room and started to put the equipment away in a huge black bag.

"Violet, you have a lot of supplies. I'm impressed," Nicole said.

Molly saw Violet put away some items that she hadn't used. "I'm glad you didn't need some of the things you brought."

Violet nodded at Molly. "I'm thankful that you had a delivery without any complications. We'll delay the eye medication so you can get to know your baby. Just so we do it within a couple of hours," Violet said.

Molly knew the eye drops were required by the state and necessary to prevent infection and blindness in babies.

"It's cool how you have a lot of the stuff like a hospital does for a delivery, but being in a home is more personal," Nicole said, as she sat on the edge of the bed.

Violet glanced at Nicole. "I have even more supplies in the buggy that I could've gotten if I had needed them."

Nicole continued, "Thank you both for including me. I don't think I'll be able to sleep tonight. Seeing the baby born was an experience I'll never forget. And everything happened so quickly." She laughed. "If I ever get married and have a baby, I want a short labor like you had, Molly. I can't wait to tell my mother how I even got to cut the umbilical cord."

Molly had been surprised that Violet had asked Nicole if she'd like to cut the baby's cord. "I'm glad you were able to be here. I was afraid Jonathan was going to have to help me deliver my *boppli*. *Danki*, Violet, for getting here in time."

"It was great to have a daytime delivery and I enjoyed having Luke drive me here. Babies seem to like to be born during the night so I usually make the trip by myself." Violet moved next to the bed and continued, "Whenever you're ready, I'm sure Luke will want to see his new niece."

"You should have Jonathan and Isaac come in here soon too," *Mamm* said. "I'm sure you'll want to breastfeed."

Molly stared at her mother for a moment, wondering if she realized how Jonathan shouldn't see her hair uncovered. He wasn't her husband. "I don't have my *kapp* on."

"You also are in your nightgown but it's fine. You just had my granddaughter. We don't need to sweat the clothing details," *Mamm* said, giving her a broad smile.

"That's right, I have my nightgown on." When Violet had arrived, she'd helped her remove her clothing so she could be more comfortable.

"The pink nightgown is lovely on you so don't worry. Even though you just gave birth, you look fine." Her mother touched the baby's tiny hand. "She is so precious and a *schee* baby. Have you thought of a name for her?"

"I like Grace." Molly wanted to use Nicole for her middle name but she decided not to mention it yet. She wouldn't want her mother to give her a disapproving look in front of Nicole. Although Nicole wasn't a plain name, Molly felt it was okay to use it for a middle name.

"Grace is a *wunderbaar gut* name for my beautiful granddaughter." Her mother left her side and walked to the door. With her hand on the doorknob, she said, "I'll go get the men and Isaac. I can't wait to see Isaac's reaction to Grace."

As soon as her mother left to get the men, Molly glanced at Nicole. "While my mother is out of the room, I have something to tell you. I want to name Grace after you and call her Grace Nicole."

Tears brimmed in Nicole's green eyes. Wiping the corners of her moist eyes with her fingers, Nicole said, "I'm thrilled you want to use my name for Grace's middle name."

Violet cleared her throat. "I know you're thinking Lillian won't like you using an English name, but you should tell her now. I doubt she'll care but if you keep it from her, she won't like it one bit when she finds out later."

"I think you're right, Violet. I'll tell *Mamm* soon." Molly decided to be on the safe side and wait until Nicole went home to tell her mother the full name.

When Molly saw Jonathan in the bedroom doorway, her heart raced at the sight of him. She hadn't noticed what he wore before when he came with his bouquet of wildflowers. Her focus had been on her hard contractions and wondering if Violet would make it in time. He looked handsome in his blue shirt and black pants.

Luke asked, "Is it okay if I put Isaac on the bed with you and the *boppli*? He's anxious to see his new baby sister."

"*Ya.*" Molly used her free arm to pat a spot on the bed next to her. "Isaac, sit here and I'll give Grace to you to hold. You have to be careful. She's tiny."

After she gently placed Grace in her son's arms, Molly watched him closely. Although she wanted bonding to occur between Isaac and Grace, she realized her toddler boy could be a little rough at times. Isaac seemed amazed to see Grace and he stared at her for a long time without saying a word. Finally, he said, "She little."

"She is but someday she'll be big enough to play with you. Won't that be fun?" At Isaac's nod, she kissed his cheek. "I love you."

Violet grabbed Luke's hand. "My husband and I are leaving to smooch in the driveway. No worries. We are quick kissers. I'll be back soon to check on you both."

Molly laughed. An Amish woman wouldn't say things like this in front of mixed company, but it was refreshing to hear Violet's amusing comments. "*Ach*, you crazy newlyweds."

Her mother grinned. "Luke, you better take your sassy wife out of here. We don't need to hear more from her."

With Violet and Luke out of her bedroom, Molly needed to get her mother and Nicole to leave. Molly wanted some alone time with Jonathan. She needed to tell him something before she lost her courage. "I'm hungry, *Mamm*. Could you bring me a sandwich? I have peanut butter spread that I made this morning."

"Sure, I'll get you something to eat. I'll refill your glass too. Did you want more apple juice? Or maybe lemonade?" Her mother picked up her empty glass.

"Lemonade sounds good. *Danki, Mamm*."

"It seems we missed supper," *Mamm* said, "but I'll fix a light meal so we can eat while you get some rest."

"That's a good idea. I can help and I'll put Isaac in his high chair so he can start eating." Nicole scooped up Isaac and followed Lillian out of the bedroom.

Molly knew how Jonathan felt about her, but she still felt nervous to tell him what she wanted. She decided to spill the important words out quickly. "I'm glad everyone left because I need to tell you something. I want Isaac and Grace to have a father so I'd like to marry you."

Jonathan studied her briefly, then said, "I hope you don't just want me to marry you so that your *kinner* have a father. I mean, of course, I want to become their father. I already love Isaac and I love you, Molly. Do you also want me for a husband?"

The tenderness in his expression caused her heart to feel as though it were turning over in her chest. "*Ya*, I do. I love you so much, Jonathan."

"How about I put our daughter in her cradle so I can kiss her beautiful *mamm*?"

He didn't have to wait for her answer because she handed Grace to him. He took the baby and carefully put her in the cradle. "Don't worry, Grace, you'll be back with your *mamm* after I kiss her."

As he sat next to her, there was a mischievous look in his hazel eyes. "I'm free next week to get hitched."

"You must spend too much time with those English fire-fighters. Amish don't rush into marriage. We need to give your family enough time to make plans to attend our wedding. I want to meet them so they can tell me what I'm getting into by marrying you."

"I can get them to come whenever you want. They will be relieved someone is marrying me."

"I thought you were going to kiss me." She didn't want to tell him that she never had gotten the memory of their short, sweet kiss out of her mind.

"I love a bossy Amish woman." He held her in his arms and slowly bent his mouth to hers.

Her eyelids closed, and her own mouth turned up to receive his kiss.

EPILOGUE

Four months later

On a sunny Friday morning, Molly looked out her parents' kitchen window at the backyard. She liked how the November frost glistened on the yard. In four days, she would be Mrs. Jonathan Mast. In some ways, the last few months had gone fast with selling her house and moving to her parents' home until the wedding. But some days had dragged while waiting to marry Jonathan. She knew he felt the same way. They were both more than ready to start their lives as husband and wife.

She noticed her father leaving the barn. *Good, he must be done with his morning chores. I timed breakfast just right.*

While she poured a cup of coffee for him, her *daed* came in. He glanced at the eggs and bacon on the stove. "This is a nice surprise. You're up early."

"I couldn't sleep, so I decided to get up. I overheard you tell *Mamm* last night not to get up this morning and you would eat cereal or fix your own breakfast. She's been working hard helping me get ready for the wedding. I'm glad she decided to listen to you."

As he washed up, she poured a cup of coffee for him. She then put a generous amount of scrambled eggs, bacon, and cinnamon bread on a plate.

"It looks *appeditlich*." He took the food and coffee from her. "*Danki*."

After pouring herself a big mug of coffee, she took a chair close to her *daed*.

He smiled at her. "I'm going to miss you when you get married. It's been *wunderbaar* having you home again."

"I've enjoyed it too. I have to admit that I was shocked when someone bought the house a few days after the realtor put it on the market."

"It was fast. That was nice Rose and Andy told you not to pay them back the money they'd given you for the house."

Rose and Andy Ebersol had helped them with the down payment. Molly nodded. "It was nice of them. They said to keep the money for Isaac and Grace. I told them they will always be a part of their lives. It's been hard on them, too, losing Caleb. I know I disappointed them when I didn't move in with them after Caleb died. They must be lonely without having other *kinner*."

"Aren't you going to eat?"

"I already ate a couple slices of bread." She exhaled a deep breath, thinking how many guests would be at their house for the Tuesday wedding. Nicole had been surprised when she'd told her how the weddings were held on Tuesdays and Thursdays in their Amish community. "It's no wonder *Mamm's* tired. I tried to keep the guest list small, but it's a first wedding for Jonathan. I can't believe how many friends he already has in Fields Corner. He also expects several friends from Kenton."

"It's fine. You both deserve a large wedding. Now that Jonathan's family are here, they plan to help. It was nice of them to invite us to Jonathan's house this evening. Your *mamm* and I are looking forward to getting to know them better. It's too bad Mary Sue and Ray aren't coming until Monday. They wanted to use the same driver as Reuben and his family."

Molly and her family had already met Mr. and Mrs. Mast a couple of days ago when they'd first arrived. "His sister, Clara, and her family are supposed to get here sometime today. I can't wait to meet his sister. Clara wrote me a nice letter after she received our wedding invitation."

"Jonathan's house is going to full with all of us plus his family."

"I'm glad Thomas and his family decided to come too. Thomas and Mr. Mast hired someone to take care of the livestock while they are away." Molly twisted her prayer tie around her finger. "Or rather Abram. Jonathan's parents told me to start calling them by their first names."

"Katrina is a pretty name," her *mamm* said, as she entered the kitchen. She wore a nightgown and her long hair was down her back. "I enjoyed the little chat I had with Jonathan's mother."

"What are you doing up?" Molly asked. "I wanted you to sleep in."

"I got enough extra sleep. When I smelled food and *kaffi*, I got hungry. I decided to be lazy and eat first before getting dressed."

Her *daed* winked at her mother. "Lazy looks *gut* on you."

"Before I leave you two lovebirds, I want to tell you something. I'm so *froh* and thankful that you two are my parents. Your commitment to your faith, to each other, and to your children has always inspired me. I realized recently that in spite of what Jeff Ankrum had done, God wanted me to forgive him. I couldn't heal completely until I forgave him. He didn't mean for Caleb to die. If you two hadn't raised me the way you did, I might not have gotten to this point."

* * *

After all the yummy food they had consumed Friday evening, Jonathan and Molly told everyone they were going to the barn to feed the horses. Molly had already moved her buggy and Cinnamon to Jonathan's barn.

"Okay, what's the real reason we came to the barn?" Molly had a feeling Jonathan wasn't just interested in taking care of the horses. She was sure he was up to something.

"I thought that was a *gut* excuse to get away from everyone. Hey, I love both our families but it's hard to get you alone these days." He smiled and took her hands into his big ones. "I have a wedding gift to tell you about. I didn't want to announce it in front of everyone."

"You already have given me too much. You're spoiling me. You bought me a new china set and dinnerware for daily use. I don't want anymore gifts." They even went and bought furniture together for the whole house. Some of it was made by Samuel Weaver. Thank goodness, she had stopped him at buying a new wall clock. She'd told him her old clock hadn't been a gift from Caleb, in case Jonathan didn't want a wedding gift from her first husband in their new home.

He rolled his eyes at her. "Look who's talking. You made an incredible quilt for our bed and made my suit for our wedding. But more important is when I marry you, I get to be a father to the two most adorable *kinner* ever."

Looking up at his handsome face, she said, "Okay, what is it? It must be really something that you can't wait to tell me until after our wedding."

"Joe, a firefighter friend of mine, said when we go on a honeymoon—"

"It won't be anytime soon. I'm breastfeeding Grace." Isaac and Grace were going to spend a night with her parents when Jonathan's family returned to their homes. She'd already started putting little plastic bags of her breast milk in the freezer for her mother to give Grace, so that they could have one night alone.

"I thought we'd go in February for two weeks. Joe's parents have bought a bed and breakfast in Sarasota. Joe showed me pictures of the place. I know you'll love it. I've never been to see the ocean and when you told me you never have, I decided we should go. Ray told me how much he liked Pinecraft when they went there for the winter. It's in the area of Sarasota."

"It sounds nice but I don't want to leave Isaac and Grace for two weeks."

"I want to take them with us. I talked to Ray and asked if they could babysit a few times so we can go to the beach by ourselves sometimes, or sightsee a little without the *kinner*. Your grandparents plan on returning to Sarasota this winter. I checked and where they're staying is close to the bed and breakfast. There are buses running all the time to the area. It's a popular spot for Amish. It's going to be our first adventure as a family."

She was touched that he wanted to include their *kinner* on their honeymoon. Even though it was the Amish way to take vacations with children, she was glad Jonathan's honeymoon plan included Isaac and Grace. She squeezed his hands. "*Ach*, Jonathan, *danki*. It will be a fun adventure for sure to go to Florida with you. And you'll get your wish."

"What wish is that?"

She smiled. "You said that you wanted to go to Sarasota before you became a senior citizen."

"That's right. I did say that. I love you, Molly."

"I love you too."

His warm lips brushed hers, and she closed her eyes, losing herself in his touch. He clutched her tightly against him. She kissed him with a hunger that caused her to suddenly break their kiss. "We better behave. We aren't married yet." She grinned. "After all, I'm the bishop's daughter. I have a reputation to maintain."

"*Ach*, is that so? I don't think Ginger and Cinnamon will tell on us."

"Okay, I'll risk one more kiss."

DEAR READER,

Thank you for reading my novel, *A Plain Widow*. While I was writing the last few chapters, we were invited to my sister's surprise birthday party. Going to Findlay, Ohio, for the party brought back many special family memories, especially about the farm where I grew up. At the party, my nieces and nephews mentioned being contacted by the present owners of my parents' farm. They wanted to let them how the Amish had asked if they could remove the wood from the old barn. Reclaimed wood has many uses such as furniture and hardwood floors. I wish I could've seen the barn before the Amish salvaged the wood, but I should've driven by it years ago.

In the past, I've said that my inspiration for writing Amish fiction came from my sweet late mother, Laoma Oberly Wilson. Her grandfather was a Mennonite minister. Hearing about the Amish at our old barn in Findlay reminded me how my dad had always liked the Amish and enjoyed talking with them. I think part of it is because he had a lot in common with them. While farming his eighty some acres, he used his two work horses to haul manure for the fields. He also hitched them to the hay wagon while I stayed on the wagon to steer them to the next spot in the field. Then he pitched the hay onto the wagon. How I wish I had pictures of my dad and me working together. However, he used his tractor for planting, plowing, and cultivating. Like the Amish, my dad loved his horses. He used the simple way of using horses for farming when he wanted, and used the more convenient tractor for other types of farm work. Combining both methods were important to him as a farmer. Obviously, being a farmer's daughter has impacted me as I write about the Plain people. My dad's love touched that part deep in my soul.

After we left the birthday party, memories flooded through my mind on the three-hour road trip back to our home. I loved our red barn and climbed the ladder frequently to the hayloft. I enjoyed looking out the large window in the loft and seeing our white farmhouse across the road. The yellow rose bush, flower beds in the front yard and my mother's huge vegetable garden looked beautiful. A close childhood friend, Diane Porter, and I used to spend time playing in the barn. She especially liked riding our work horses.

I've included an excerpt from my historical Christian book, A GIFT FOREVER. It has many elements in it from my childhood. It isn't Amish fiction but is a wholesome story about a family who value and support each other.

Blessings,
Diane

AN EXCERPT FROM
A GIFT FOREVER

PROLOGUE

It was 1957 when I saw something I wasn't meant to see. I have never forgotten this night because it had such an impact on me. I was only seven years old, and what I saw my father doing confused me. Finally, I had enough courage to ask my mother about it. After she explained everything to me, I was shocked and saddened.

What happened after I learned my father's greatest secret was extraordinary to our family. When my father, Justin L. Reeves, decided to conquer an overwhelming disability in life, he was fifty-four years old. He gave our family an incredible gift to last a life-time because of what he accomplished at this age.

His triumph made me into the woman I am today. My three older siblings were able to make the best decisions of their adult lives because of our father's influence.

This is a story of determination and hope. My father's journey was not easy. But if it had been easy, I wouldn't be telling his story now. After you finish reading this book, I pray the true meaning will linger in your heart and mind; just as the outcome of my long ago memory has remained in my soul for fifty-six years.

My name is Debra Reeves Cunningham, and I am sixty-three years old. It's not hard to take you back to the beginning in 1957 when I was seven. My life was good and simple. My memories of this wonderful year are crystal clear. We lived on a farm with eighty acres outside of Findlay, Ohio. My petite mother, Lucille, worked hard doing whatever needed to be done on the farm. She was a big help to my dad when it came to dairy chores. With no milking machines, they milked eight cows by hand in the morning and again in the evening.

My siblings didn't help with this time-consuming job. My oldest sister, Gail, was twenty-five and lived at home, but not by her choice. Whenever she mentioned moving to an apartment, our mother insisted that wouldn't be proper for a single woman. Gail worked as a secretary at the impressive Ohio Oil Company in Findlay. She always dressed in pretty clothes and went out on dates all the time.

My brother, Carl, at the age of twenty-one was in the Army and he hated it. He wrote me the best letters. The past summer, we all traveled in our blue Mercury car to visit him in North Carolina.

Next in the family was my fourteen-year-old sister, Kathy. We shared a bedroom, and she never complained about sharing a room with a younger sister. She only worried about not being able to dance. From the time she was a small child, she wanted to be a dancer. She watched all the Shirley Temple movies and practiced on the kitchen linoleum floor. I was told how her dancing entertained me when I was a fussy baby with teething pain.

A short time after Kathy celebrated her seventh birthday, she was stricken with polio. She wore a brace on her left leg because the polio had weakened her muscles. Dancing was no longer a realistic dream for Kathy.

It's time to take you back to the night when what I saw made me question everything. From my siblings, I learned that sometimes we see only what we want to see, and only face the truth when we can no longer deny it. I remember everything about that night so well. In my mind I see my bare feet softly walking down twenty-two steps. I enjoyed counting the steps and jumping off the last one.

It drove Gail crazy whenever she was in a hurry and behind me. "Why do you have to count these stupid steps all the time?"

"I like to count them. I always get twenty-two."

And so on this particular night I counted them again. With no light on to guide my footsteps, I didn't want to fall in the dark. I didn't switch the hallway light on because it would shine through the register. My parents might wake up and see the light from their bedroom. Mommy liked to keep a door open for air circulation in their small room. I knew I had to be very quiet since I wasn't supposed to be up at this late hour. I skipped the jump off the last step so my parents wouldn't hear me. With a racing heart, I slowly opened the old stairway door, hoping it wouldn't make a sound.

CHAPTER ONE
The Secret

I opened the door at the bottom of the stairs just enough to slide through, and released a deep breath in relief the door hadn't creaked. My mother would continue sleeping.

Loud striking noises in the dining room startled me. I stood still, counting the bongs of the grandfather clock. The striker stopped at twelve. Oh no, it must be midnight. If Mommy heard me, she would want to know why I was up at this late hour. I had to go pee but hated to have to tell her this. I could hear her say, "Debra, I told you not to drink so much before going to bed."

My parents slept in the downstairs bedroom next to the kitchen and dining room. I needed to go through the kitchen to get to the only bathroom.

I tiptoed across the dining room floor toward the kitchen. The old door wasn't shut tight, and a narrow band of light shone through the crack. Someone was in the kitchen.

Rats. It's probably Gail. I didn't want to see her. She would tell me about her date, and what a great time she had. I always wondered if her dates ever got to talk. Gail was some talker, and poor

Kathy was the one Gail usually confided in. But Kathy was asleep, so Gail would want me to be her captive audience. Then Mommy would be sure to know I was out of bed.

I got to the door and peeked through the crack. Our kitchen was large with a high ceiling. Blue-flowered paper covered the walls. I had pasted the long strips of wallpaper for my mother to hang.

My green eyes stopped at the small cabinet where my mother's homemade fruit pies set on top. Mommy had just baked them that day. I remembered I hadn't eaten any pie for supper. Maybe I could go pee, and before going back upstairs to bed, I could pretend to listen to Gail while eating a piece of pie.

My gaze shifted to the far side of the room. We ate our daily meals in front of a picture window with white ruffled curtains, and my eyes widened when I saw Gail wasn't in the kitchen. Daddy was at the table, still dressed in his gray work clothes. Why wasn't he in bed? What was he doing?

Opening the door a little wider for a better look, I saw a yellow pad on the table. I watched Daddy copy words from my reader to a page in the tablet. Why was he copying words from my new book?

Mommy purchased this extra book for me to have at home in the summer for practicing my speech. School would start soon and Mrs. Garrison would be my second grade teacher. Daily we worked on my pronunciation of the words in the text so that when I read the same pages in school, the teacher and my peers would understand me. I couldn't remember Daddy ever looking at it.

Before I could leave my spot and ask why he had my book, I saw his lips moving. He softly spoke, "D-a-u-g-h-t-e-r." After he said the letters, a look of confusion crossed his face, and he rubbed his chin.

I wanted to go in and ask him why he was copying words down and why my book puzzled him. Something held me back. For several minutes he copied words while I twisted my long, dark brown hair around my finger.

He sighed and closed my book. I watched him pull open a bottom cabinet drawer, lift the towels, and place the tablet underneath. He closed the drawer with the tablet hidden. It's a secret, I thought.

Although I didn't think he would enter the dining room, I moved with quick steps, hiding behind a big chair with a slipcover over it. I was relieved when I heard the bedsprings sink with his weight. After I heard his snores, I hurried through the dark kitchen to the bathroom. Finally I got to pee.

I quickly washed my hands with little water. I didn't want the noisy water pump to alert my parents I was up. Wiping my wet hands on my pajamas, I walked past the cabinet, then turned, and went back.

I need to see the tablet.

Since I didn't want to risk having the kitchen light shine in my parents' bedroom, I took the pad into the bathroom. I turned three whole pages of words printed in a shaky handwriting. Tonight wasn't the only time he'd copied words.

Muffled laughter scared me, and I swiftly returned the tablet to its hiding place. Before going back upstairs, I listened at the open window to Gail talking softly to her boyfriend, Phil Dunsmore. I saw they were in each other's arms on the porch swing.

Should I ask Gail about the tablet? Gail's chatter stopped when Phil kissed her on the lips. Now was not the time to bother my sister.

When I climbed into bed and snuggled next to Kathy, I realized my daddy didn't know he had spelled daughter. How sad he didn't recognize this word when he had three daughters. *Maybe I should wake Kathy and tell her what I had seen and heard.*

But I decided to keep quiet and think about it instead. For once in my life, I wasn't anxious to find out what was happening in my family.

Amish Sloppy Joe Recipe

Ingredients

1 lb. ground beef
1/2 C chopped onion
1 tbsp. Worcestershire sauce
2 tbsp. brown sugar (packed)
1/2 C ketchup
1 tsp prepared mustard
1 tbsp. vinegar
1 tsp salt

Directions

Brown meat and onion, drain and return to skillet. Add remaining ingredients and simmer for 15-30 minutes.

Number of Servings: 4

This is similar to how my mother made sloppy joes except she never used Worcestershire sauce, mustard, and vinegar. I usually make it like my mother did. I love to put pickles and a slice of tomato on my sandwich.

CRESCENT EGG AND SAUSAGE CASSEROLE

Ingredients

2 packages of crescent rolls
1 lb. ground sausage
10-12 eggs
2 cups shredded cheddar cheese
salt and pepper to taste

Preparation

1. Preheat the oven to 375 degrees. Lay 1 package of the crescent rolls in the bottom of a greased 9 x 13 casserole dish, pinching edges together as needed. I spray the bottom of the Pyrex dish with Pam.

2. Cook the sausage in a skillet until browned, seasoning with salt and pepper as desired. Drain fat.

3. Meanwhile, scramble the eggs in a medium skillet (don't cook them through completely, since they'll be finishing in the oven). I just salt and pepper the eggs.

4. Layer the sausage, egg mixture on top of the crescent rolls in the casserole dish. Top that mixture with the scrambled eggs, then sprinkle with cheddar cheese.

5. Roll out the second package of crescent rolls and place on top of the cheese. Cook for 11 to 13 minutes according to directions on the crescent roll package, until crescent rolls are lightly browned.

CPSIA information can be obtained
at www.ICGtesting.com
Printed in the USA
BVHW072242261118
534073BV00001B/207

9 781544 735894